MY BOSS, MY DESTINY?

TANTALIZING WORKPLACE ROMANCE.

ANGELA CASEY

Angela Casey

My Boss, My Destiny?

Tantalizing Workplace Romance.

Also, by *Angela Casey.*

My Boss, My Destiny?

1

KARLA

Karla tossed and turned in bed at night on her first day at work. Any time she closed her eyes to sleep, all she would dream of was her boss, Mr. Jake Soles. What is happening to her? This instant attraction she felt the moment they met. How could she nurse these feelings for a man who went on a rant on her the minute they met? Finally, she slept in the wee hours of the morning.

Her first day at work was nothing but eventful. The last thing her father said before she left the house on her first day at work was what he always said when she was starting a new job.

"Get it done right, Karla!" he exclaimed, a twinkle in his eye. It was just her luck that her dad would add a dash of pressure and humor to the moment, as if implying that getting it done wrong was not an option unless she wanted to face his wrath and a lifetime supply of dad jokes.

That had been her plan since the mail came one hot Sunday after church. CBBR Group, Inc. had hired Karla to work as the Paralegal/Secretary to a brilliant lawyer in the company, the CEO, who was the son of the company's Chairperson. It was a dream come true, the kind of opportunity that made her pinch herself just to make sure she was not trapped in an episode of "The Office."

It seemed okay that she had spent hours getting ready in her room that morning. When she saw her reflection in the glass door while entering the CBBR building, she knew it had been time well-spent. Her white shirt was crisp and contrasted nicely with her checked tailored pants and black high heel shoes. With just the right amount of hair gel, she had managed to tame her usually bushy brown hair into submission, transforming it into an up twist that would make Einstein envious, well, maybe not quite.

"Hi Karla," a voice interrupted her thoughts. When she turned to look, she found herself face to face with William Carol, her boss's assistant. He took her hand firmly into his, giving it a shake that threatened to dislocate her arm. Karla wondered if he had secretly been training for a world championship in "Handshake Powerlifting."

“Good morning, Sir,” she tried not to make her smile too tight, although her face muscles were already putting up a valiant struggle, desperately trying to maintain a friendly expression while silently begging for mercy.

He waved off the greeting good-naturedly, as if dismissing the formality of it. "Mr. Soles, our boss, is not in today. He is away at a conference out of town. But that does not mean a free day for you. In fact, the boss has an entire month booked with court cases."

Karla's mind raced with possibilities. But before she could delve further into her daydreams, William's fast-paced speech snapped her back to reality. It was like he was on a mission to set a world record for the fastest verbal delivery.

"You already know your job description as a Paralegal/Secretary, but to get you started, I will run through what you job will consist of here."

Karla struggled to keep up with his words, feeling like a marathon runner attempting a sprint while wearing clown shoes. She mentally cursed her decision to wear high heel shoes instead of flats.

“You will deal with research. Miss. Mr. Soles is very keen about his records. You will have access to very confidential documents. You will take care of—"

Karla's ears perked up at the mention of "confidential documents."

"And one more thing," William interjected, breaking her from her secret agent fantasies. "Mr. Soles expects excellence. He is not one to tolerate mistakes or mediocrity. This is not just climbing a mountain. It is climbing Mount Everest with a blindfold and one hand tied behind your back."

Karla suppressed a laugh. Mount Everest? Blindfolded? It seemed a bit dramatic. She could not help but picture herself in a climbing harness, blindly reaching for footholds while juggling case files.

She mustered up the courage to respond, her voice a tad shaky but laced with humor. "I understand, sir. I will do my best to meet Mr. Soles' expectations. Should I bring my climbing gear tomorrow?"

William raised an eyebrow, a flicker of amusement in his eyes. "Well, that would certainly make things interesting. But I think we will stick to the legal office kind of climbing for now."

Karla chuckled, relieved to see a glimmer of levity in William's demeanor. "Good to know."

They both shared a brief laugh, breaking the tension that had lingered in the air. Karla felt a surge of confidence.

She realized that she could navigate the treacherous terrains of this job with a bit of humor and a light heart. Because she could not even remember what he had said his name was, she did not think she would remember everything he rattled off on. There was no time to take out a notepad either, so she would have to do her best.

"As I said earlier, you would be dealing with research. Miss., Mr. Soles is very keen about his records. You will have access to very confidential documents, I am sure you know. Mr. Soles does not tolerate lateness and disappointments, so have his materials ready before he needs them. He could send you packing if you make errors on reports or drafts. Look, Mr. Soles has a particular way of doing his job and it is not like any way you have ever known and guess what? He does not care. It is best you figure it out on your first day. CBBR did not find its way to the top through a ladder. We did mountain climbing. Everything you think you have earned and are worth, triple it three times and that is a quarter of what Mr. Soles is worth. Try to do a good job so that you do not lose your job before you get your first check is all I am saying."

Karla felt palpitations in her heart as it started to beat fast.

The man did not notice or offer any comfort. He stopped abruptly in front of an office, took out keys from his pocket and pushed the door open.

"The files on the table are all you will use to work until the boss is back. It is self-explanatory but if you need help, give me a call, or just come over to my office."

The name tag on his door said William Carol. Hers had her name on it. The overhead clock in her office ticked to 10 am as William's door clicked shut.

Karla, though new to this kind and caliber of job, was

not new to working. She had been working since high school. She had part-timed a variety of jobs. Being this nervous about a new job seemed strange to her.

The office she now occupied was the office of the former Paralegal/Secretary. There were files already arranged into the filing cabinet. She scanned the office to see if her predecessor left a hand over note, but she found none. Karla now knew she was on her own.

Karla wasted no more time. She got behind the desk immediately. She picked up the first file and her eyes scanned through its content, a report. The next was another report. *What was she supposed to do with them?* The third document was a draft. Then it clicked, he expected her to get them arranged in the file cabinet behind. It was just a guess.

It did not take a while before she straightened up, *done.* The clock said she had only spent thirty minutes at it. Karla furrowed her brow. Her gut told her that this was not all she had to do before the boss returned. Resigned, she went over to William's door and knocked. The door opened immediately because he was already on his way out.

"Just the person I wanted to see," he said, "Good news, you may meet the boss today." It seems like William had a way of making good news sound scary. The razor-winged moths in her stomach that were just beginning to settle came alive again. William raised a brow and tipped his head toward her office. She got the question in them immediately.

"I have completed arranging the files, sir," Karla told him.

"Arranging?" His raised brow turned to a frown. The moths were vultures now.

"You are supposed to compare the drafts with their

respective reports, crosscheck them with other available files to ensure that the information tallies. The boss will require them as soon as he is returns and you must hand them over in order of importance."

"Order of importance, sir?"

William sighed, as though she was being stupid.

"The boss's schedule is available in your office."

It was? She had not done more than glance around her office since she entered.

"You will work with that and arrange the files according to the ones he needs soonest. That is the order of importance."

Was that the standard for self-explanatory?

She had woken up this morning thinking that she was the most blessed girl in the world but now, she was struggling to keep that same point of view. Karla only managed to mutter a 'thank you' before she disappeared behind her door.

William was right. Near to the filing cabinet was a board and stuck to the board with a pushpin was the boss's schedule. Karla carefully detached it from the board. It would be helpful in locating the files she had arranged. She hurried over to the cabinet, praying that she recognized the ones needed. Kicking her heels off, she dragged her leather swivel chair out and sat down.

The next time she looked up from her work was when a beep alarm went off. She figured it was for her lunch break though the time was past lunchtime. It was 3:20 pm. But the footsteps she heard in the hallway convinced her that just like everything else in the office, the habit was different. She stretched now, realizing that the file she had just shut was the last of them.

A knock came on her door just then and she softly responded, "Come in."

"Karla, what are you still doing here? The boss rang for you minutes ago!" William sounded genuinely worried.

Karla scrambled to her feet, slipping into her heels, while picking up the files. She followed William, but it was already too late. The boss was standing just at her door, his other staff behind him.

No one needed to tell her who he was. He had the aura. He was tall and handsome, and stood like the world's most formidable emperor. His suit was impeccable. Her hands trembled and her heart skipped. He mesmerized her until his arrogant voice brought her down to earth.

"Miss Karla Bronson, they told me that you were good enough for this job and I am already disappointed. Workers are known to bring their A-game on their first day and if this is yours, I doubt you will be here long enough to get your first paycheck."

His dark eyes pierced hers and all the pores on her skin, all at once, in a flat, yet threatening stare. His voice was flat, not deep but had a depth that went down to the vultures threatening to eat her up from the inside.

"I am very so-" she began.

"Here is one piece of knowledge to keep you on-board here longer, 'sorry' fixes nothing. Take it from someone who must work with cases a thousand and one heartfelt apologies could not fix."

The back of her eyes stung.

He stretched his hand out to her, and she would have been clueless if someone at the back had not signaled to her to hand him the files.

He took them from her and shuffled them.

"Where is the draft for Thursday's case?" he asked.

Where his face had been expressionless, it was now full of irritation and anger.

Had she not taken it out of the filing cabinet? Her memory refused to do her any favors now.

"I'm so- I will bring it to you immediately, sir."

Karla did not wait for a reply, she ran into her office and to the cabinet. How could she have missed a file? She had used the schedule. She tried to recall the number of files she worked on. She only remembered working with ten, which she had just given the boss.

She heard footsteps go past her door and figured they were tired of waiting for her. How discomforting it was that the boss had scolded her in front of so many people and in front of her office.

She nearly tore apart files, searching for the one file.

"Karla, I was particular on the 'order of importance,'" William said, walking in.

"I know, sir and I was. I do not know what file the boss is referring to."

"The Blackjack case. It is a particularly important and confidential case Mr. Soles has been working on all year." William's information was detrimental to her nerves, especially considering how strange the case name was to her.

"I submitted ten files, sir."

"Ten? Were there only ten files on the table? Are you sure you did not mix anything up?"

"I cross checked sir."

"Are they all the cases for this week?"

She nodded. "I did not see such a name on any file."

William covered his face with his hands. "That was what she was referring to," he muttered to himself. Then he turned to her. "The previous Paralegal/Secretary

did not hand it in."

"Where is she now? I could go pick it up," Karla offered, hope and a little bit of relief pouring in.

"Nowhere we can go."

Hope and relief disappeared.

"The boss will be livid."

Despite this file loss turmoil on Karla's first day, Mr. Sole still noticed the exquisite beauty of his new assistant. She possessed luscious bushy brown hair waves that he instinctively wanted to grasp. Lips that yearned for his kiss or so he imagined. And she had a body that sent his imagination into overdrive. He wondered if fate was toying with him. He had not felt this instant attraction about a girl since college.

2

DEDICATION

The last thing Karla learned that afternoon was that if anything were the boss's job, it would be her job too. That included errors that were not even hers in the first place. The last Paralegal/Secretary should have handed over all the files with a written handover note. All that did not matter. She is now in charge. She could barely breathe now, standing next to a worried William. The ache that had been in her stomach was now in her chest and her head.

"You must speak to Mr. Soles. You told him you will report to him at once," William reminded her.

"He is already upset with me. I am not sure he has enough patience left with me. It will only be worse if I am the one to tell him about the files," Karla replied, her voice filled with uneasiness.

"It is your job as his Paralegal/Secretary, Karla."

Karla thought she felt her heart rate triple. The air conditioning was not doing any good as beads of sweat were now rolling down her face and soaking up her shirt. Even though she tried hard not to show her uneasiness, she knew it was impossible.

"There must be something I can do. I could search the office for it. She must have misplaced it," Karla said, getting down on her knees and searching the cabinet for anything that had the name 'Blackjack.'

It would be hard to find a document she had never seen or knew anything about. But the thought of getting Mr. Soles any angrier seemed harder to bear. She could feel her hair coming out in strands from the elastic band she used to hold it. Her job was not the only thing falling apart.

"Karla, there is little chance that you would find it in the office. There are over a thousand files to look through and little time for you to do it," William explained, his tone filled with resignation.

"Is there any way I can contact the previous Paralegal/Secretary?" Karla inquired, not looking up from what she was doing. It was best she ignored how much it seemed like she was unjustly taking the blame for the former Paralegal/Secretary's mistake.

"I am afraid not. CBBR has a policy not to contact former workers, except under very necessary conditions."

What, Karla wondered, does the fact that a confidential and soon-to-be-needed document had gone missing, not count as "a very necessary condition"? Resigned, Karla straightened up and began to walk, heart in mouth, toward Mr. Soles' office. His office was the one at the end of the hallway, and his name tag was on the door in bold letters. Karla turned to see that somewhere along her walk, William had fallen back, turned around, and was now retreating into his office. She took another deep breath and knocked once.

"Come in," she heard him respond.

She walked in, feigning calm.

He looked from her face to her empty hand, a question in his stern eyes when he looked at her again.

"I was not given the file for the Blackjack, sir," Karla said, her voice clear as she wanted the words to sink in.

"William confirmed that he gave you all you needed. That file is the most important one of them all. It contains the drafts, reports and all the information I need for the case, including all the progress reports I reviewed," he was standing now and coming toward her.

"All of that was not handed to me, sir," Karla said clearly, as though she wanted the words to sink in before he came any further.

"I do not think you understand the gravity of what you are saying, Miss Bronson. You do not understand the worth of that single file. The Blackjack case is a three-year-old case. That file contains not just all that history but the conclusion of each court hearing. We have had a year to work on this current case. We cannot show up in court on Thursday empty-handed. Do you even know what that means for CBBR?"

He had stopped moving but he was not too far away from her now. She could see the dismay and anger in his gaze, the irritation in the way the corners of his eyes crinkled and the self-control he was holding on to in his clenched fists. "Look, Miss Bronson, CBBR has not had a dreadful day in court in years. You cannot come in and change that. I do not care what you--" he swore under his breath, "did or did not get from the former Paralegal/Secretary, but do not give me a reason to take drastic measures. We have until Thursday."

Karla kept her gaze on the man, it was all the show of confidence in herself she had left. She knew he could see she was unhappy. She was not wrong, only unlucky. Her eyes searched for any kindness she had hoped the man who was now walking back to his seat, had. She could not find it in his creased forehead, furrowed brows, his pinched nose and tightly shut eyes, nor in his clenched fist.

When he spoke again, she could tell he had reached his last and thinnest shred of patience. His voice was slow, low, and strained. “You are part of CBBR now. If it crashes, I am holding you responsible.”

Somehow, she knew it was her queue to leave. It was miraculous that she could find her feet and that they were able to walk. The tears were going to come any moment but were not going to look any different from the sweat on her face. She shut the door behind her and kicked her heels out again. She was certain now that wearing them had been a bad idea.

She did not know what to do. It was 5 pm and the other offices had closed. It was past closing time already and anyone who could offer any help or advice would have already left.

A knock came and William poked his head in.

“Quite a wacky first day, huh?”

“Quite?” She replied.

“Hey, anything I can do to help?” he asked.

She was upset, so she shook her head. She said, “Thank you, Mr. Carol. Could I please have all the records of the Blackjack case?”

He nodded and pointed to one of the cabinets she had not noticed.

“The good news is that what is missing is just the draft for the Thursday hearing. Every other Blackjack file is available in there.”

Karla concluded that she and Mr. Carol had different views of what good news was.

He handed her a piece of paper. "That is my direct cell number. Call me if you need anything."

He was on his way out. Her stomach grumbled, a reminder that all she had had all day was a slice of toast and coffee on her way out in the morning. The nerves had made it worse.

She waited till Mr. Carol's footsteps had receded before she stepped out to find somewhere to get something to eat. She took the elevator to the last floor since she still was not familiar with the place. The ground floor was scanty, and she tried to avoid eye contact with people, not wanting to encounter anyone for a pity party on the grounds of what had occurred earlier with her boss. In the end, she settled for just a bottle of water on a table and coffee from the coffeemaker. Once she set down the water and coffee, she found herself in the Blackjack case cabinet. She took each file out, one after the other, checking the date for each one.

All she found were reports and drafts for past dates. There was a flash drive, too, which she immediately inserted into her computer. She found that it contained recordings of previous court meetings of the Blackjack case. What she needed to do stared her in the face, impossible as it looked. She was going to create a draft for the boss. She must listen through the recordings and read the files for history and accuracy's sake.

She only remembered as an afterthought to call her family to inform them she was going to work overtime. Sips of coffee and a series of deep breaths later, she got to work, playing the recording at extra speed. She listened keenly as she made notes. Her hand moved at Godspeed and her eyes scanned through documents even faster. She was tabbing up and hoped they would come through on track changes. By the time she had made any real progress, the sky was so dark outside that she thought she had closed the curtains. Her body was beginning to war against any further stress too. Even coffee could not fix that. She looked at the clock and gasped. It was an hour to midnight.

3

REGRET

Jake Soles put down his phone for the third time in one night and waited another twenty minutes for sleep to find its way to him, yet no sleep. His mind wandering. He had a busy morning ahead, and he needed to sleep very desperately but despite how tired his body was, he was still very awake. His thoughts were all over the place.

He had a particularly trying day from the moment he got to the conference. Everyone else was late and he had arrived an hour early. At the end of the conference, they had not been able to make any headway on the issues on the table. It had taken all his morning and half of his afternoon. Then somehow, he had gotten stuck in an hour-long traffic jam.

He had heard that his new secretary had begun work that day and was hoping that she was able to cover for what he could not complete in the morning. Then he had walked into the office, and she was not responding to his calls. That was enough to get under his skin after his difficult day and lofty expectations.

Jake thought to himself, it is a lie when I told her she was good enough. She deserves more credit than that. She came highly recommended, but for someone called outstanding, I expected better than a report that the file disappeared into thin air. But hey, he reasoned, it is her first day on the job. Maybe, she has magic tricks up her sleeve which will manifest later.

Deep down, he had to admit that there was something about Karla that stirred up his emotions. *I could not stop staring at her or fantasizing about her! Fate is toying with me. I have not felt this way about a girl since college, my first love in college. What could go wrong? Everything. Now, Karla has entered my life and even with her bad first day at work, she is already wreaking havoc on my sense of peace. I am in trouble.* Jake rubbed his eyes in frustration.

He felt a sense of guilt for the way he had treated Karla, and it was keeping him awake. "I'm going to have bags under my eyes in the morning. Maybe I should have taken those Yoga classes to learn how to find inner peace," he grumbled, sitting up in bed. Jake sighed and decided to take a more forgiving approach. "I need to be nicer to Karla, show some remorse for my actions. And as for the missing file, well, I will wake up with a genius idea in the morning. Or I will just keep dreaming about Karla, who knows? What is happening to me? Why does this girl have this effect on me?"

With that resolution in mind, he tried to calm his racing thoughts. It was not fifteen minutes later when he fell into a deep slumber. Hopefully, his guilt would fade away.

When Jake's guilt still lingered, he began to worry. But his worry turned into joy when he walked into his office the day after the incident to find out that Karla had worked all night and miraculously provided a new Blackjack case draft for his court proceedings on Thursday.

"Well, I will be damned," Jake muttered to himself. "Karla, the secret overnight superstar. Is she on a mission to prove me wrong? I must say that if is, she is doing a pretty damn good job."

Jake could not fathom how Karla had managed to accomplish so much while still finding time to go home, sleep, change clothes, and make it to work early.

His initial conclusion was that Karla was trying to make up for her mistakes and impress him. "Classic over-achiever syndrome," he chuckled. "I have met many girls like that in my lifetime. Always trying to prove something."

But as time went on, Jake's view began to shift. Karla did not seem like the type to seek validation. "In fact, she is proving to be quite the enigma," he thought, scratching his head. "Either she is a master of indifference, or she genuinely does not care about impressing me. And that bothers me more than it should. She is definitely mysterious."

As Jake's thoughts continued to spiral, he could not help but feel drawn to Karla despite the obstacles between them. *Apologizing might be a good start*, he mused, watching her walk briskly toward him. *Although knowing me, I will trip over my words and end up apologizing for something completely unrelated. For example, 'Sorry for that time I accidentally stole your pen in kindergarten.' Smooth, Jake. Smooth.*

But as Karla handed him the Blackjack case file, she seemed unfazed by his grateful smile or the conversational tone in his voice. "She is a tough nut to crack," Jake grumbled, feeling a mix of frustration and intrigue.

Little did Jake know that Karla had her own reasons for maintaining her distance. Yes, he hurt her with his rant on her first day at work, but she cannot fool herself. There is an undeniable attraction between them. Her father's words of caution echoed in her mind, reminding her to be wary of executives. Even if she learnt to navigate Jake's arrogance and her employment status, the social class divide would remain a big obstacle. She must just remain professional. She must stay away from him.

He must never know the number of times he appears in her dreams, both walking down the street hand in hand and gazing into each other's eyes. In the office she would not even look into his eyes for fear her eyes would betray her. She would not text him unless it is about work.

Jake stared after Karla as she walked away, a mix of confusion and amusement on his face. "Maybe I am just reading too much into this," he chuckled to himself. "Or maybe I am slowly losing my mind. Either way, this woman has certainly made an impression on me."

With that thought, Jake turned his attention back to his work, determined to find a way to bridge the gap between them and his intriguing secretary, Karla.

4

DISTANCE

Karla felt her hand burn where hot coffee from her cup had spilled over and scalded her. She smiled sheepishly at the lady behind the coffee dispenser. It could have been worse like it had been last week. Mr. Soles had given her access to his own kitchen. It is now her responsibility to bring him his lunch.

It was not part of her job description, so she had seen through what he was trying to do. Mr. Soles, she observed, was not a horrible boss as she had thought on the first day. But since that incident on her first day at work, he was determined to ensure that she saw the good side of him.

It was why she was stuck with bringing him lunch when she went to get her own, because he constantly offered to get hers. It had its upsides and downsides. The upside being that she could bring more food home to her family. The downside being that it took so much more out of her as it was more work.

On more than one occasion, he had demanded a meal that she had never heard of in her life. It was not surprising though. Her life had not been a dramatic one until she started working at CBBR. Before then, she had not known life away from South Loss Angeles, where she had spent 23 years of her life.

She had grown up in a family of five, including her parents, George and Pricilia Bronson. Her father never earned much as a gospel preacher and her mom was a homemaker. So even before high school, life had forced Karla to grow up too quickly to survive, with more responsibilities than kids her age.

To help support her family, she had worked part-time jobs ever since high school and even made it through college on scholarship, more part-time jobs, and student loans.

It was a demanding thing to do. Her parents taught them that their background was not a valid excuse for failure.

But that week, settling for Googling the recipe for that food, she wondered if her background was a good excuse. Working with Mr. Soles was like living on the opposite side of where she had grown up. She and Mr. Soles were worlds apart in manner, lifestyle, and opinions. She did not know too much about him other than common knowledge, but the little she knew solidified that fact. It was purely divine inspiration that she had come to work at CBBR, one of the largest real estate firms worldwide, directly under the Chairman's son, Rodney Soles.

The only thing she and Mr. Jake Soles had in common was a workplace and the fact that they had both worked extremely hard to arrive where they are in their lives despite their backgrounds.

At the end of last week, she had politely asked Mr. Soles to employ a chef for his cooking. The straw that had broken the camel's back was that Mr. Soles himself had walked in on her at lunch trying to figure out how one of the appliances worked.

Thankfully, he heeded her request, and she had walked in that morning to find the new chef at her post.

"You must be the boss's new chef. I am Karla, I am his Paralegal/Secretary."

"Yes, I am Marie. The boss mentioned you would come. He wanted to know if you came for coffee yet," Marie said.

Karla raised her brows, surprised but said nothing, only nodded and went away. Better not to raise suspicion. She did not know what that was about. Was the boss trying to assess her? Had it all been a test and she had assumed it was a show of regret? She did not want to think much of Mr. Soles. She was working hard at her job. She did not even give him cause to complain. Just last week, CBBR had sealed a major deal based on a draft she had written.

This week, she showed up at work at exactly opening time, hoping that by the end of the day she would conclude record research she had been working on.

She shut the office behind her, put down her coffee and got to work at once. A minute later, her eyes fell on a document she was supposed to give to the boss. She picked it up, sighing. She wanted to see less of Mr. Soles. All she wanted to do was get her job done. Unfortunately, her job especially required working with Mr. Soles ninety percent of the time.

Karla knocked on his door and waited.

"It is open," she heard but the response come from behind her, and that startled her.

She had been absent-minded and had not heard him come up. Now she whirled around and came face to face with this incredibly good-looking man. She almost lost her balance, but he caught her. For a moment, their eyes locked, then he released her.

She blushed and stuttered, “Go --od morning, sir.”

“Open the door,” he smiled and gently said.

She did and he let her walk in first before he shut it behind her.

“Good morning, Miss Bronson. That was quite a start,” he smiled, and if he expected a certain reply, she would give him a different one.

“This is the contract file for the Devon Plot, the legal office assigned this case to you” she said, handing him the file.

“Is that for the Netherlands office?” he asked.

“Yes. It arrived in the mail recently and I worked on it. All you need to do is sign it and I will mail it back, sir,” Karla said.

Jake considered seizing this opportunity to start a conversation about them, but he missed the chance. The two doors came together with a soft click of magnet, and she was gone.

Karla was filling his thoughts more than he wanted to admit. Jake knew he was everything women wanted and more. It is not conceit. It is a fact. His days in school and afterward had proven just that. His charm, intelligence and wealth had kept women around him for so long. In fact, he had gotten into one or two affiliations, none of which lasted long, all because of who he was and what he had. Yet, Jake had never allowed that to get into his head.

When he began to work at CBBR, he had a strict rule of not getting involved with any of his staff. Not that any of them had come so close.

Then Karla showed up.

Mr. Soles was a keen observer of even his own emotions. He had not worried when he felt guilty for scolding an employee, it was not the first time. But when the guilt became more pronounced, he took note of it. That was unusual. He fought to get rid of it.

He thought that if he compensated her for his actions, it would be all. But all that had done was bring her closer to his thoughts. Worse still, she was standoffish. She acted like she did not know it, but he could bet she knew the game she was playing. She played it well with her perfect poker face and indifference.

She made him want to notice her. But if he knew this, why was he not able to ignore her as well? Why was he so interested in knowing if she was happy? How did he somehow know her routine so well?

There was something about her that got on his nerves but in a way that he feared he was beginning to get addicted to. It was not like him to think of a woman so often.

What was so different about a woman whom he clearly knew was playing hard to get?

Jake scribbled his signature, as he signed the documents, hoping that the thoughts of Karla would disappear.

5

TRIP TO WASHINGTON

Karla had been working at CBBR Headquarters for more than six months now. She has settled in well. Her indifference to her boss, Mr. Soles, has paid off as their relation now is a perfect boss/employee relationship. If something was heating up in their hearts, it remained hidden and unexplored. She was enjoying her job.

It was so on this beautiful spring morning. On her way to work, she noticed the cloudless sky, the Pacific Ocean in the distance, the mountain ranges, and the cityscape . It reminded her of her high school days, how they went on day trips to check out the newest blooms of spring wildflowers. She had seen PoppyCam at Antelope Valley. She had also seen fiddlenecks, slender keel fruits, red maids, and forget-me-nots, at the Antelope Valley California Poppy Reserve. All of these helps make spring in LA so beautiful.

Today, things were not going well at the office.

The next call came in as she hung up on the last.

"Hello, I am Karla Bronson calling from CBBR Headquarters. I would like to make a last-minute reservation for two rooms at your hotel?" After a pause, "Wow, it is all booked? All right, thank you."

Karla had a hand to her forehead, fingers tapping lightly, frustration beginning to creep in. How could she have made such a costly mistake?

Somehow, she had overlooked the detail to bring an extra at the end of an invitation and had only reserved one VIP suite which was for the boss. Everything was set for the trip the next day when Mr. Soles told her that she was his plus one. As his Paralegal/Secretary and his personal assistant, she must be the staff to go with him on this trip. The legal office had already asked Mr. Carol to represent him elsewhere.

She bit her lip until it got painful. Mr. Soles was specific about the hotels he found comfortable. She had called all of them, only one was yet to reply and that was where all her hope hung. The hotels were sold out and no rooms were available.

If worse came to worse, she would have to book a motel for herself, whichever one was closest to the hotel, even if it meant making an extra effort to meet Mr. Soles during the trip.

Her phone rang and she reached for it.

"Hello?" she said, without looking at the number.

"Miss Bronson."

"It is Jake."

She hid her apprehension and responded professionally.

"I remember you said you have reservations already for me, but I will need to collaborate with you before the conference. Please ask the hotel to reserve neighboring rooms for both of us. I do not mind if it means paying extra."

Her day could get worse unless she told the boss that she reserved only a room.

It was not something she ought to tell him over the phone, but he had already hung up, so Karla stood there perplexed. *What hat trick was she going to pull off to make sure they both had reservations for a 3-day conference?*

By the evening, when they were both boarding CBBR's official jet and on their way to Washington DC, Karla still had not been able to pull off any magic act. She, also, against better judgment, had not told her boss that she had only reserved a VIP suite at Continental Hotel. It had beautiful décor and a pleasant water view. She did not even want to bother about the per suite rate. She was simply happy that it was one of the hotels Mr. Soles liked.

She was determined to spend the flight bracing for whatever was to come.

"Miss Bronson."

It was the way he stressed her name that made her know he had been trying to get her attention for over a minute.

"I am sorry, sir. I got a little distracted," she said.

"A little?" he chuckled, taking a cracker out of the snack box between them. "First time flying or just terrified of heights?"

"Both," she replied, a funny look on her face.

She looked so worried, Jake thought. He wanted to tell her about his first time on a plane, but he did not remember it. He had been flying since he was a kid. Instead, he picked up a magazine and returned with his cracker to the seat opposite her.

"Mr. Soles," she burst out a minute later, nearly startling him, "I messed up our reservations and only got one for you. I have been trying all day to secure a second one, but I was unable to. I am still trying to find a nearby motel that I could stay in for the trip duration."

The words rushed out all at once and there was an awkward pause after them as he tried to understand everything she said. She waited for the outburst.

"First of all, Miss Bronson, it does not look good that an active CBBR employee, especially an executive, stays at a motel."

She was surprised that he was keeping calm this long.

"Secondly, wow. All right, do you mind staying in my room?"

"And where would you stay, sir?"

"My room, of course."

Now her eyes widened.

Four and a half hours later, they had gotten off the plane and had checked into their hotel room. The Elevator ride to the suite was very awkward and quiet. Now they were both standing inside the VIP room looking around awkwardly and silently.

JAKE BROKE THE SILENCE, "Okay, so this is not the suite where they have two beds. It is just one king-sized bed. Well, we can still make it work." He walked towards the bed and continued, "I could sleep on this side while you sleep at the other end" "Aha!" He grabs two pillows from the bed and placed them in the middle of the bed as a demarcation, "See! Easy! It is two beds now, nothing to worry about. Come in and unpack," he said while walking towards his luggage and dragging it to his side of the bed. Karla did the same.

Karla had finished unpacking. Thankfully, there were two separate closets. She picked one and Mr. Soles picked the other one. She was ready to leave the room and eat dinner. She knew she had to wait for him. She might have waited for a lifetime because he had been trying to fold his clothes for about thirty minutes. He had folded and re-folded, but he was still not satisfied.

She decided to offer support, in the form of advice, "Uhm. Mr. Soles, why do you not hang them instead?" He turned to her and said, "I want to hang some clothes and fold some. That is how my housekeeper arranges my clothes in my closet."

She smiled, stood up and walked over to him. She stood in front of him and took the shirt from his hands, for a minute, their hands touched. Karla felt a shock go through her. She did not understand why her body reacted that way, so she quickly turned away and started to fold the shirt.

Jake stood there and watched her till she arranged all the clothes.

He walked towards her and stopped when he was in front of her, he looked into her eyes and said, "You did not have to do that, but I do appreciate it. Thank you, Karla." Karla's heart was melting. What was happening? His eyes were burning into hers and she suddenly became hot. She did not know how to control these feelings, so she quickly stepped away.

"It is fine. I am glad that I could help" Karla said.

"Well, we have not had anything to eat since we arrived. Let us have dinner," Jake insisted as he walked towards the door. To Karla's surprise, he opened the door and ushered her out before he followed suit. She had observed this sort of curtsey twice now. She felt a certain warmth in her heart.

They had a quiet dinner, but Karla did not hesitate to notice the stares that Jake gave her, when he thought that she was not looking. *What did this mean?* They made her very conscious. After dinner, they discussed the itinerary for the next few days and Karla played with her hair subconsciously while talking. That was something she did when she was flirting.

An hour later, they were back in their suite, and ready to call it a night. There was just one problem. They both needed to change into their pajamas.

"Okay, You can make use of the bathroom, while I change here. That is fine with you, right?" Jake asked her. She nodded in agreement. She grabbed her pajamas and her toiletry bag and walked to the bathroom. She could not believe what was happening. The mistake she made was the reason she and Mr. Soles were sharing a room. She failed to do her job well. Instead of being mad about that, Mr. Soles had been very calm and nice towards her.

The reservation was not the only thing she had messed up, Karla thought. She must have gotten a different Mr. Soles, too. It did not make any sense that he was the same man she had met on her first day of work. She wondered what had changed. She could not say it was the trip that made him kind to her. Mr. Soles had been particularly easy-going with her for a while. In fact, she could not remember any time, except her first day at work, that he had been mean to her.

Karla wiped off her makeup, put on her night moisturizing cream, took off her dress and changed into her pajamas. She gathered the dress and the toiletry bag and walked back into the VIP bedroom. She stopped dead in her tracks, when she saw Mr. Soles, standing with his bare chest, he only had his pajama pants on. He was staring into his phone, so he did not realize that she had returned to the room.

Karla stared. She looked at his chiseled chest. They

looked like they belonged on a Greek god. The way his arms flexed as he texted on his phone sent shocking waves through her body. She could not lie to herself. She loved the sight. Although she knew she should not, she could not help it.

Jake looked up at her and that was all she needed to snap out of it and put her things away.

She got into the bed and laid her head on the extra pillows they had asked for at the reception, because they had used the ones the hotel had initially supplied to create the demarcation between them on the bed.

"Goodnight Karla, please get some rest" Jake said to her as he also settled into bed. This was the second time today, that he had called her Karla. What did it mean?

"Goodnight, Mr. Soles" she replied. Immediately, she heard him say, "Please, call me Jake."

The next morning, Karla woke up with her palms on something hard, yet warm. *What was that?* She thought. With her eyes still closed, she tried to figure out what she was touching.

Shocked, she turned after she realized that she was touching Jake's chest. She pulled her hand away quickly and covered her face. "I am so sorry" she mumbled. "That was not intentional."

SHE HEARD JAKE LAUGH, "That is perfectly fine. You wanted to grab the pillow and did not realize that while you were sleeping you had thrown it off the bed," he said in a calm tone. When she realized that Jake did not mind, she opened her eyes and sat up, but she still did not make eye contact with him.

Jake stood up from the bed and continued, "I am at fault

here. I am sorry. I hate to sleep with a shirt on. I did not consider the fact that you were also here, and that you might feel uncomfortable. I will just wear one now," he walked to the closet and grabbed a shirt and Karla could not stop staring at him, at how his back muscles flexed while he stretched his hands to wear the shirt. What was happening to her? And why did she have to be in this position? She still had to spend two more nights with him.

"I am ordering room service for breakfast. Tell me what you would like. I know yesterday was stressful for us both. So please, eat and rest. Then we can both get ready for the meetings later," Jake said to her while walking towards the phone. She did not understand why he was doing this. He was very caring towards her and that made her heart flutter.

The breakfast was great, served with the hotel's signature fruit juices, blended with the freshly roasted coffee aroma.

They had the first meeting and after that, they proceeded to eat lunch at the hotel's restaurant. He talked to her about the case, which surprised her. He talked as if he valued her opinion about the case. He asked her what she thought about his strategies on previous cases. They talked about his career till it was time for the next meeting.

A short while later, they had wrapped up their meeting for the day. Jake cleared his throat and said, "It is time for dinner. There is this nice Indian restaurant I go to whenever I come to Washington. I would love to take you there."

Jake studied her face and quickly added, "I promise, the food is great." Karla agreed and they stood up and left.

When they got to the restaurant, Jake had made sure they sat in a comfortable spot, where he knew they could be alone, and no one would disturb them.

They designed this Indian restaurant with bright jewel

tones mixed with fiery earth tone. This created rich palettes and a visual sensation. The plates and table mats matched this visual. With the matching furniture, the restaurant exuded Indian/ Asian decor. The attentive waiters dressed in Indian outfits but spoke perfect U.S. English.

Karla had confessed that she had never had Indian food before, so he ordered for her. They both had garlic Naan bread and lamb curry.

"Okay. This tasted good. Thank you for bringing me here." Karla said after she finished eating. He nodded at her with a wide smile. She had never seen him smile this way. He looked so good. She looked into his eyes, and they locked gazes until the waiter interrupted them with the bill. Jake knew that dinner was over, which meant that they could go back to their room and call it a night, but he wanted to spend more time with Karla. He wanted to talk to her and get to know her.

"I knew you would love it. In fact, I have a funny story about this place," Jake said, and Karla urged him to tell the story.

He told her the story of the first time he went to the restaurant as a little boy with his mom and how he had cried because the restaurant did not have chips and burgers. Karla laughed at the story and went ahead to tell a funny story from her childhood too.

"When I was young, I did not believe the fairy tales my mom told me of the moon being cheese," Karla said. The corner of Jake's lip curled amusingly but he said nothing. "I thought that someone threw a tennis ball too high up and then God seized it."

She laughed when Jake snorted to stifle a laugh.

"I have to hear more of these things you came up with," he remarked, his dark eyes sparkling with attention.

They spent the night laughing and sharing stories over a bottle of wine.

Mr. Soles, Karla discovered to her utmost surprise, was a funny man and had a sophisticated sense of humor.

She had also found that he was allergic to mushrooms when he told the story of how he broke out with rashes all over his face and body after he ate mushrooms at a restaurant. They rushed him to the hospital.

Mr. Soles told her about horses and food recipes over dinner. Though he spoke as though he was reciting a business plan, she found out that he knew how to hold an enjoyable conversation. He let her pitch an idea for business. It was amazing how all of that made her relax.

The next day, they ate dinner together again. This time it was macaroni and cheese because he had let her order and that was all she yearned for. That is the food she has enjoyed since childhood, and she was comfortable with.

The moon was directly over his head, The hotel's dining room showed a magnificent view of the sky through the transparent ceiling and the relaxing water view.

Karla continued with her childhood stories and could not help but chuckle at Jake's reaction. It was refreshing to share her childhood imaginations with someone who found them amusing rather than dismissive. She took a bite of her macaroni and cheese, savoring the warm, cheesy goodness.

"Well, there was another time when I was convinced that vegetables were from another planet," she confessed, a mischievous glint in her eyes. "I mean, think about it, they come in all sorts of weird shapes and colors, and they magically grow from the ground."

Jake laughed heartily, a genuine and infectious sound that echoed through the dining room. "That is quite an imaginative theory you had there, Karla. Who knows, maybe there is a vegetable mothership hidden somewhere out there."

They continued to share stories and anecdotes, their laughter blending with the pleasant ambiance of the restaurant. Karla felt at ease in Jake's company, appreciating the way he embraced her quirks and engaged with her stories.

Later that night, as they were walking back to the hotel, Jake noticed that Karla was feeling cold. She had worn a dress with short sleeves and the night was chilly. He stopped, took off his Jacket and held it out for her to wear. She refused, "Oh no! I am fine. Thank you." Jake insisted, "Please put in on, Karla, I cannot watch you freezing and do nothing about it." She put on the jacket, and they continued walking.

Jake wanted an excuse to touch her, and he produced one, "Well now my hands are cold," he said. Then he held her hand. Her hand was soft and fit perfectly into his. His skin was burning and tingling, he felt warm in his heart. For the first time in a long time, he was not just lusting after a woman, but he was having feelings for her, like a little schoolchild.

Karla could smell him all over the Jacket, and she knew that the warmth she felt was not only because his jacket covered her. Her heart was also skipping ten times a minute. As she was trying to control it when he held her hand, suddenly, her legs became weak.

Ten minutes later, they were back in their VIP suite. She returned the jacket to him. She thanked him for an amazing night and for his jacket. He thanked her too for being good company. She took off her shoes. She had been wearing heels the entire day, so her feet felt sore. She started to massage them. She was getting a bit of relief, but she did not really know the best way to tend to the sore spot. Jake watched her and walked up to her,

"When I was little boy and I wanted something that I was not allowed to have, my mum would make me do silly things, before she would give them to me" he sat next to her and continued, "Like one time, when I wanted a scooter. She said she would only buy it if I did something else in return, I agreed. Then, she took off her shoes and made me massage her feet." Karla laughed and asked, "As a kid? I am sure you declined and ran away."

Jake shook his head, "Nope, I wanted the scooter, so I spent about five minutes rubbing her leg. And that became our trade pattern." He pointed at her feet and continued, "You are doing a really terrible job, so let me help you."

Karla did not know what to say, she could share a room with her boss, wear his jacket, and hold his hand. But let him massage her feet? She could not let him do that.

"Oh no! You have done a lot for me already, thank you," she said politely rejecting his offer.

"This is just my way of saying 'thank you' for trying Indian food today, please let me do this for you" Jake responded.

Karla knew that she had lost, so she nodded, agreeing to Jake massaging her legs. Jake grabbed her foot and got to work. The massage was so good that Karla almost let out a moan. When he finished massaging her, she thanked him. He smiled. They stared at each other, and Jake's head inched a little closer to hers, she looked into his eyes, and as their eyes locked, she could see a longing in his eyes. He was so close now and just when Karla thought he was going to kiss her, he stood up and thanked her again.

Well, she must have misread what that was, she thought to herself. She went into the bathroom, wiped off her makeup, put on her night cream, and changed into her pajamas, while Jake stayed in the room to change into his pajamas. They got into bed and said goodnight. Though the pillows demarcated them, both slept with the thought of each other lingering in their minds.

Jake continued extending nice gestures to her. He took her to other restaurants and shared more stories about his life. It felt like this trip was all they needed to become closer.

Just when she thought it could not get any better, he had gotten a city tour for them to see the beautiful scenery of Washington DC, a beautiful city with impressive architecture and spectacular scenery. Viewing many scenic views with him filled her with a renewed wave of national pride: the memorial to George Washington, our nation's first President, the Lincoln Memorial, the most beautiful structure with a prominent location on the National Mal and the Jefferson Memorial, and a dome-shaped rotunda that honors our third president. The spring cherry blossoms' bloom illuminated the city. The tour narrator was good, but Mr. Soles gave her additional commentary that she wondered how he knew something about everything.

The highlight of the trip for her was when Mr. Soles directed the question thrown to CBBR at her, on the second day during the conference. It was not just about the show of faith in her but the squeeze he gave her hand when she sat down was something else. That, and the nods she got from other people present assured her that she had spoken well.

As they left the dining room on the last night of their trip, Karla glanced up at the moon, its glow casting a gentle light on their path. She felt a renewed sense of wonder, knowing that life was full of surprises and delightful moments, even in the most unexpected places. And as she walked beside Jake, she could not help but look forward to the next chapter of their adventures together, both in and out of the office.

When the trip ended, a new relationship had developed between Jake Soles and Karla, a new sense of belongness, and togetherness. "Would she dare to call it a "mutual development of feeling?" She discovered that not only was his boss a good man, she felt that she could also trust him.

6

CHANGE

Karla Bronson had never played golf. She only knew what it looked like on the sidelines in college. She was not sure of the right way to hold the golf club. Nor was she sure what had made her accept the invitation to watch Jake play.

The Soles' security agents led her to the exact spot in the family's resort in the Santa Monica Mountains where his parents lived, and where he had grown up. He was the host. She remembered he had mentioned that to her. She spotted him on the golf course and gave him a shy smile. He nodded in recognition and made a gesture to the two guards he had sent to her. He wore a white tee shirt, shorts, sneakers, and a white face cap that was a stark contrast to his black hair. Karla felt that he looked even more handsome in this sports outfit.

For miles and miles, all she could see was the green landscape and trees on the golf course. There was also space for the audience. The guests' tables were for two or three and they had brought partners.

Though there were not too many watchers, golf certainly was something important among them.

During one of their conversations, Jake had told her that he had been playing golf since college and he had held the trophy for all the years he was in college.

She was excited to watch him play, though she did not know anything about the rules. She had told him that when he invited her.

"The game will be fun to watch, trust me. It is a 9-hole round so it should not be longer than two hours," Jake said.

The game began and she watched keenly.

Jake was the first of three players to take a shot. He walked up to the line marking and fixed his tee to the ground. Then he set his ball and picked out a club from his bag before setting it aside.

Though Karla's attention was on him, she could not help noticing the kind of people around. Jake's family had affiliations with their own caliber of people and that was not surprising. She wondered if his family was in the crowd. She wondered who the people were.

Her vantage point only allowed her to see him from behind. She watched as he swung the club and it connected with the ball kicking it off the tee.

Someone nearby let out a low whistle.

She was too distracted looking at Jake to watch for where the ball landed. Jake walked off the shooting mark to an applause from the crowd.

Karla hoped that no one noticed the confused look on her face.

Jake's eyes roamed the audience for her and when it settled on her, he gave a small smile. Thankfully, he turned back to his game before her cheeks turned pink.

As the third man walked to his turn, golf carts began to

arrive. She had not spared a thought as to how they were going to keep on watching when the players and their balls were out of sight. When the audience began to stand and get into carts, Karla blended in and found herself a cart. Jake, she knew, was farther down, having gone to find his ball.

The carts came to a stop where one of the men found his ball.

From where she was, she could see Jake waiting by his own ball. She had also just realized that the golf course had obstacles.

Golf, Karla thought, *was certainly the kind of game she would expect Jake Soles to love playing.* If she did not know any better, she would have thought that everyone present was just a version of Mr. Soles.

They trained their eyes to be able to watch the course even while they engaged in conversations. It was surprising for Karla to hear the details they were able to talk about, gesturing and pointing and making commentaries.

She was lost in thought, wondering how she got acquainted with Mr. Soles. She marveled at how she became his guest.

During their trip to Washington, she had finally decided to let go of her first impression of him.

Her biggest surprise had been the fact that he did not scold her for failing to reserve a second room. He found a way to share the room and ward off questions from the press who were already curious about their relationship.

It was honorable that he found a way to manage it without alerting her. She would not have known if one of them did not directly approach her to ask questions.

Jake Soles made her feel comfortable all the way. When she had casually mentioned that she missed the lunch time they spent together, he had admitted that he had enjoyed it as well. A week later, he invited her to have lunch with him while they discussed business plans.

It was not until she spent time thinking about it that she realized that CEO Jake Soles was not just a boss anymore. He was now her friend.

She did not have to be nervous whenever she walked into his office. She had learnt that grace was not an excuse to cross the line. So, she never let their friendship affect her professionalism.

That has kept their friendship going smoothly so far. Then, he had invited her to watch his game.

Her attention returned to the game now to see that they were all close to the hole. As her mind wondered she had no idea how long she had lost concentration, while the driver assigned to her golf cart carried her along.

It was Jake's turn to swing. He wasted no time in doing that.

The ball ran a distance, veering a little off the straight path she had expected it would take to the hole then slowed down. Her attention moved from the ball to Jake's expression.

It was characteristically Jake.

Jake's emotions were easy to miss. It was one of the first things Karla had noticed about Jake since they had begun hanging out.

She had found that his true emotions were mostly in his eyes and in the way his body moved. Even when it appeared still, it moved.

She was glad that she could see his eyes from where she stood outside her cart. He looked up, found her at once and smiled. She could see the excitement in his eyes.

It was that, not the soft applause that came a nanosecond later, that told her he had just won the game.

She raised her hands and began to clap, mirroring the smile on his face. Jake came towards her.

“I am going to be honest with you, I did not understand half of how the game worked," Karla admitted, giggling.

“I saw you a couple of times,” Jake replied, taking out a club.

"I am glad you spotted me amidst all of these people," Karla said, grinning. "Though I must confess, my knowledge of golf is limited to what I have seen in movies."

Jake chuckled and stepped onto the green, readying himself for his swing. "Well, do not worry, I will give you a crash course in golfing 101. Just remember, the objective is to hit the ball into that tiny hole over there," he pointed to a distant flag, "using as few swings as possible."

Karla nodded, trying her best to absorb the basics. "Right, got it. So, it is like a fancy version of miniature golf?"

Jake raised an eyebrow, a playful smirk on his face. "Well, let us just say it is miniature golf for grown-ups with more rules and fewer windmills. But do not worry, I will make this mini tutorial of 'golf' fun for you."

As Jake prepared to take his swing, Karla positioned herself near the edge of the green, excited about seeing him display his golf skills. She watched intently as he swung the club, sending the ball soaring through the air.

"Wow, that was impressive!" Karla exclaimed, clapping her hands. "You make it look so easy."

Jake grinned, walking over to join her. "Thanks, but it took a lot of practice to get to this point. Golf can be frustrating at times, but it is all about finding that perfect balance between strength and precision."

Karla chuckled, leaning in closer. "Well, if it is any consolation, I can be your official cheerleader on the sidelines. I promise not to offer any unsolicited golf advice or distract you with chants of "Go, Go, Go!'"

Jake laughed, appreciating Karla's lightheartedness. "I think having you as my cheerleader would make the game a hundred times more enjoyable. Just do not be surprised if my shots miraculously improve with your presence."

Though she had gotten lost in thought, she had never taken her eyes off him and could even narrate his game play to him.

"Do you have plans for later this evening?" He inquired unexpectedly.

Karla shook her head.

"Then let me treat you to my celebratory dinner, anywhere you want."

Karla stifled a smile.

"There is a place I walked past on my way here. Their food smelt nice."

"Dolores. I am sure that is the place. So, I will see you at 4 pm?"

"5 pm is better. I need to jog home and shower."

"Let me give you a ride," Jake offered. He saw something flash too quickly behind the look she gave before she declined politely. He knew not to insist. She turned around and began to jog.

She did not jog too far when she stopped a cab and took a ride home. She could have used the ride home, but she was not ready to accept that much from Jake regardless of how close they had grown. She also did not want to make her family, especially her father, worry. She had not forgotten his advice, 'stay away from the Executive.'

It was not the first time he had invited her to dinner. The first time, something had come up for both at work and they had to stay back and finish it. At the end of it, they were both so tired that they made do with coffee to keep them going until they went home.

As agreed, Jake met Karla outside of Dolores. He wondered why she had not chosen any of the bigger or more well-known restaurants.

Was there a possibility she still did not feel comfortable with him? After their trip, they had started to talk more often, and the relationship had shifted to more than just a boss-employee relationship.

He adored her company, he did not even mind what his ego had to say about the admission. Karla was smart, hard-working, and conversational. He loved her sincerity. It made him feel at ease. It was easy to trust her. He did not have to worry about gold digging as he did with other girls in the past.

There was still a tiny part of him that feared that Karla would one day turn out to be like them. But that part bowed to the part of him who wanted to tell her everything about him just to watch the way her eyes lit up or the tiny nod she gave when he spoke about his ideas.

She sat in front of him now, in a long black dress with a jacket. The image of her when he had spotted her stuck in his mind: her brown hair in an impossible bun, her eyes the shade of moss, and beautiful fair skin. The way the gown hugged her perfect figure made him think of a dream he had long forgotten.

"You mean you were not homeschooled?" she asked.

"No, I always assumed that people from your background did not have to struggle like the rest of us," Karla said.

He shook his head, delighted at her surprise. "Never. My father believes that school is meant to take you outside your comfort zone to teach you to survive. So, I attended private schools, graduated summa cum laude in Business Administration and Management, completed my JD at Harvard Law School - -"

He stopped suddenly, a stray thought crossing his mind. Did he sound like he was bragging?

Karla remembered what she had read about him, when she was preparing for the interview for the job. Jake Soles was born and raised in a wealthy family that lives in the Santa Monica Mountains, a neighborhood of the rich and privileged. He attended private schools and graduated summa cum laude in Business Administration and Management Studies and completed his JD at Harvard Law School. His father, Rodney Soles, is the Chairperson of CABR Group, Inc., a holding company that conducts all operations through its indirect subsidiaries. The Company is a commercial real estate services firm that has four hundred offices worldwide.

Jake Soles did not only distinguish himself in academics, but he also played golf and played basketball in college.

He searched her eyes for any telltale sign.

She frowned.

"What is wrong?"

Her gaze was so pure, he nearly lost his words. He had never been so unsure of himself, even when he had to take the winning shot for his college basketball championship.

"Did I offend you?" Jake asked.

He decided to be honest with her, "Well, talking about the things I have done or places I have been, might sometimes come off in the wrong way. I know I was born into privilege, but I never want that to be what fuels my conversations. I am sorry if I sounded that way."

Karla looked at him intensely, she was shocked that he was apologetic over something that he did not do. She did not think he was bragging and felt the need to reassure him, "You have massaged my feet before, Jake. That is about as humble as one gets. Whatever conversations you have with me, I am fully aware of what you mean." She could see the relief in his eyes.

Jake was so happy that she knew him so well, and he really enjoyed hanging out with her, he wanted more, "Do you have a free Saturday? What do you say I take you to the beach?" he offered.

He is an only son doted on by a loving father who expects perfection from him.

Though six foot tall and extremely handsome, friendly with girls, he has never had serious relationships, except his first love in college. People say he sees most girls as gold diggers. Judging from his looks, achievements, and family background, he must be one of the most eligible bachelors in the city of Los Angeles.

After working for five years at a famous law firm, he decided to accept a legal and management position at CABR Group, Inc., as a legal Counsel and CEO. The Paralegal/Secretary assigned to him was a middle-aged woman who decided to retire a month after he assumed office.

Then a beautiful young lady, Karla become his Secretary.

Jake was indeed a talented and privileged man. Why would him saying the obvious offend her?

Noticing her silence, Jake said, "I am getting very fond of you and would like to spend more time with you."

When Karla just continued to look at him shyly, he asked again.

"Do you have a free Saturday? What do you say I take you to the beach?" he offered again.

"What is your favorite relaxation spot?" he asks.

"I cannot decide between Saturdays at the beach and chess." He added.

"I never thought I would end up close to someone like you. Chess is relaxing to me." Jake added.

"You were the nerdy kid, let me guess," Karla finally said.

"I was not. I played basketball. I was quite the lady's man." He spoke.

They laughed.

Karla rolled her eyes dramatically, but she could not say that was hard to imagine. Not only was he handsome, but Jake Soles was, also the most eligible bachelor in town. In fact, she had been surprised when she discovered that he was still unmarried.

There was no obvious reason. He had the looks, the riches, and achievements to his name. She could vouch for that. Surely that sent all sorts of women his way. The way his hair fell over his eyes was enough to make a person stare.

"I will meet you at the golf course on Saturday. Then we will go to the beach," Jake said. Karla shook her head in agreement.

It was Saturday and Karla got ready. She met Jake and they went to the beach. When they got there, Jake led Karla to a spot. She was surprised to see that there was a blanket on the sand along with snacks and drinks. It looked like a picnic, a picnic by the beach. This gesture touched Karla and she wondered when he organized all this.

"How did you do all this?" Karla turned to look at him, waiting for a reply.

She saw a hint of a smile play on his lips. She loved seeing him smile. It made her heart feel very warm. It brought her so much joy. He looked into her eyes intensely, "I just wanted to do something nice, I want you to always remember this beach experience."

She felt a surge of happiness. She offered him her hand, look into his eyes, and said, "Let us look around."

Like newly minted lovers, hand in hand, constantly glancing at each other, they perused Santa Monica beach. The sprawling beach was over three miles of soft well-groomed sand. The line of palms on top of the high bluff, the sky-blue ocean water with waves and a view of the Santa Monica skyline, filled their hearts with joy. Families and children running rounding around, playing, and the surfers added to the happy atmosphere. It was serene.

At the end of their walk, they sat down on the blankets on picnic by the beach area. Jake handed Karla a board game, scrabble, and challenged her to a game, stating that the loser would get dinner for the winner. Karla accepted. She loved a good competition. They ate their snacks and played the game, they laughed merrily, especially when Karla argued that BIET was a word.

"I mean it is like diet, but with a B, it is sort of like the opposite of diet" Karla argued while giggling. Jake laughed so hard that he placed his hand on her thigh for support. Karla stopped laughing. She looked at his hand on her thigh and looked into his eyes, Jake did the same. He looked into her eyes, and he let his eyes roam her body, he looked at her beautiful body accentuated by her bikini that clung to her every curve. He wanted to taste her skin so bad, his eyes went down to her thighs, where his hand was, and he imagined using those hands to caress her whole body. He dipped his head to taste her. He looked up at her lips and imagined how they tasted.

Karla felt a longing in every part of her body. She wanted him. She knew that. She wanted his hands to explore her body. Without looking away from her lips, he said in a raspy voice, "Let us get back to the game."

She sighed when he took his hand off her thighs and she continued the game.

The game ended with Karla as the winner. She did a happy dance which made Jake smile and watch her. They talked a little more, had their remaining snacks and drinks and they stood up and packed up the blanket.

"So, I guess I owe you dinner, Karla" Jake said as they walked back to his car.

"Yes, you do, and I want to have the tastiest dinner ever. I need tasty food. Really tasty food." Karla said while patting her stomach, which made Jake smile at her. Jake had a plan to cook for her. What he never told her was that he had trained as a chef at a Michelin restaurant in Paris, France, when he was younger and interning in Paris. He spent a year learning how to cook amazing dishes and he wanted her to taste them. So, he lost the game on purpose, just so he could get a chance to cook for her. He did not want her to know about the part about losing on purpose.

When they got to the car, Jake spoke, "I trained as a chef in France and I make the most amazing meals, so I would love to cook for you tonight. Is that okay?" Karla looked at him, she was surprised. But she was also eager to see him cook and taste his food. Oh! That also meant that she would be over at his house, alone, with him. She is an adult, she reasoned. They spent three nights together alone in a hotel VIP room in Washington not too long ago. What could go wrong? She agreed.

They got to his house, and she admired how minimalist the decorations were, it really showed his cool personality. They got to the kitchen, and he led her to a seat on Kitchen Island. He grabbed his apron and put it on. He walked towards the refrigerator and brought out a steak wrapped in a plastic bag. He also grabbed potatoes from the shelves and vegetables from the refrigerator.

He looked at her, "Today, chef Jake will make caramelized steak and garlic mashed potatoes" he said and bowed, this made her giggle.

She watched him cook the steak and just when he was about to add salt, he made a funny gesture by folding his hand like he was about to throw a basketball.

She laughed so hard, because she knew he was referring to a trendy internet video about a chef. She watched him cook the steak, boil the potatoes, and steam the vegetables. She watched as his arms flexed while he was mashing and stirring the potatoes. She was hot and it was not because she was in the kitchen. Parts of her that she did not know were on fire. This man attracted her, and her body wanted him.

Jake plated the food and placed a bottle of red wine on the table. They ate and drank the wine. Karla hummed when she took the first bite and the look of approval and happiness on her face pleased Jake. He loved that he had satisfied her. He wanted to keep satisfying her in every way possible. He wanted her. All of her.

They finished their meal, and he took the plates to the sink. They continued drinking their wine while he answered all her questions about his time in France. Karla was curious as to why he went to learn to cook in France.

"I love cooking and I love to see the satisfaction on people's faces when they taste my food, now, especially yours." He said that last part while he moved a little closer to her. Jake looked into her eyes, and he could see that her longing mirrored his. He wanted to tell her how he felt because he was tired of keeping it to himself. He wanted her and he was not going to waste any more time.

"I have feelings for you, Karla. I cannot help it. Thoughts

of you consume me. I want you, all of you. I need you. I understand if you do not feel the same way, but I cannot keep it a secret any longer. I want to satisfy you in every way possible and I need to know if you want that too." Jake confessed.

Jake's confession stirred something in Karla, and she moved closer to him and crashed her lips into his. They kissed like they had been starving for each other for so long. Karla came up for air, "I have feelings for you too, Jake. You make me burn. I want you so bad and I have wanted you for the longest time." Hearing this drove Jake wild, he lifted her and placed her on the top of the kitchen Island. He kissed her again, this time letting her know how deep his hunger was, he traced kisses down her neck and went back up to her lips. He sucked on her ear lobes in between whispering sweet nothings into her ears. He raised his hands and grabbed her, finally able to feel the lushness of her. He traced the kisses to her cleavage and looked up at her with such passion. In one swift move, he unbuttoned her top and drew her to him in a firm hug. They squeezed tightly in each other's arms. They tasted the passion and fire between them. She moaned loudly with her eyes closed. He traced his tongue till he had her lying on the kitchen Island. He kissed her neck. He planted his tongue all over her body till she was moaning so loudly. Her whole body was shaking with passion. Then he brought her to a sitting position and kissed her, but suddenly, she gently stopped him.

"I love you Jake, but I am sorry, I cannot go all the way, Jake. I want to go all the way only with the man I marry. I am sorry," Karla said. Jake felt like someone dumped a bucket of ice on him.

"I understand but is there a reason. I mean, did someone hurt you?" Jake asked with concern etched on his face because he saw the longing in her eyes too. He was certain that she wanted him too. He had read of women who never wanted to be intimate with a man because of experience of abuse. He would kill anyone who caused her such pain.

"Oh no! I am the daughter of a pastor, and it is outside our values. I am sorry," Karla said.

Jake understood and nodded. He gave her a quick kiss on the lips and brought her down from the kitchen Island. They spent time talking a little more and then he drove her home.

Out of curiosity, he asked, "Are you saying that you have never gone all the all with anyone before?"

"No, never. I love you. If any man would take me there, it would be you, " she replied.

After hearing that, he smiled as he became happy again. He planted a long lingering kiss on her lips, and said, "we will do as you wish."

7

MOTHER'S INTERVENTION

The sun was working to set the world on fire when Mrs. Soles ordered her driver to start the car and head for CBBR headquarters. The sun was not even as hot as her temper.

She could not make sense of the all the rumors she had heard about her son, Jake. While she had paid no attention to such rumors at first, thinking it was not possible. This morning she discovered that she was wrong. She looked at the photos in the newspapers. That is Jake and his Paralegal/Secretary.

"It is about Jake," her friend had said to her over a call, sounding grim.

No one hated fake news like Stella McGerald, head of L.A.'s bestselling women's magazine. It was Mrs. Soles' second cue to pay attention apart from the fact that they were friends, and their children were even closer friends. Stella's daughter, Marie, used to be one of the girls Jake spent his time with before he got so busy with work.

Stella told Jane that people had seen a certain girl that had been going out with Jake to beaches and restaurants.

She told her of how she watched them sit together for hours at the beach, laughing and conversing. Earlier, Jane had ignored rumors of a new face at the golf club. She now suspected that must have been the same girl.

Jane requested information about the mystery girl. It was not long before she had her answer: Karla Bronson, daughter of George and Priscilla Bronson, who no one knew about. She was her son's new Paralegal/Secretary who, in Jane's opinion, was quickly trying to seduce her son, Jake.

She knew too many girls like that, and Jane was worried that her son was already smitten with the sugar-coated vision of her, she must have crafted for him. The streets coughed up these kinds of girls. She was not going to sit back and watch a skillful actor named Karla scheme her way into her family's hard-earned wealth. This sort of thing did not happen in her day. Marriages in her circle were either encouraged or allowed among people from wealthy and famous families that belonged to the upper social class.

She was even more hurt when her husband, Rodney Soles, refused to share her view on this issue. But that did not matter. She was going to fix the problem. She was her son's mother. She had a lifetime responsibility of watching her son's back, being his eyes when he was too distracted. It was like the time when he was younger and addicted to chocolate, his teeth be damned. She had soothed him when he cried but unrelenting when he craved the sweets. He was grateful when he got older, and he would be grateful later once he saw she had saved him again.

She knew how hard he had worked for CBBR. Karla could not just prance out of nowhere and steal all of that from her son.

Jake did not need to know she was pulling strings on his behalf. Certainly, not anytime soon. It was going to look as natural as possible. As quickly as the girl had come out of nowhere, she was going to disappear fast, and far away from her son and his work.

Jane herself was going to be there to wipe her son's tears if they came. Better he cried now than later when he would have lost the so-called love and his money.

She canceled her entire schedule for the day for this reason. It did not matter how long she spent in the traffic they were now stuck in. She was going to ensure that Karla was out of her son's life this very day.

She sat back now and tried to calm herself before she met the despicable Karla.

Karla Bronson returned to her office after walking her CEO downstairs and into his car. He was not going to be back at the office till the next day. If she did not have to work on his draft for an important case coming up soon, she might have agreed to go with him to the conference as he had wanted.

He had invited her to have dinner with him if she got off work early. She looked forward to it. Sharing a meal with Jake had fast become the highlight of her days. Not only did she enjoy their conversations, but it was also a joy to listen to him speak. His voice always had a soothing effect on her. He often shared stories about his college days, his basketball and golf competitions, his trips to other states in the U.S. and overseas. He often ended with words like, "I will take you there someday."

She had barely sat back in her chair when the alarm went off. Karla raised an eyebrow.

Did the boss return already?

Had he canceled a meeting to make it to dinner with her? He had done it once, to her mixed reaction of dismay and pleasure.

She stood, already trying to feign a stern face so she could effectively admonish Jake about what canceling meetings meant for the business.

William, who had formed a disturbing habit of not knocking, poked his head through the door.

"Hello Mr. Carol, Mr. Soles has returned?"

"No, miss," he paused, a frown on his face, "Mrs. Soles, the boss's mother, just called to say she will be coming in today."

"Alright then. Do we need to prepare anything for her visit?" Karla asked.

"Not exactly. She has not come to the office in over a year and now she calls to say she will be here in a couple of minutes." William replied with a frown on his face.

"We do not know why she is coming here today, do we?" Karla asks.

"She mentioned something about seeing her son's new Paralegal/Secretary," William replied, his frown lines deepening.

Karla could not say she was not surprised by that. She did not want to be worried. It is possible that Jake had mentioned a thing or two about her to his mom. She was Jake's mom. But again, Jake would have mentioned it to her if he had told his mother, *would he not?*

Mrs. Soles' car pulled into the main building. They heard footsteps.

Karla turned around and William was gone. She brushed the front of her skirt, not knowing what to do with her hands. She was nervous.

She counted seconds until she heard the bell on the door leading into the corridor of her office. Mrs. Soles was near.

Mrs. Soles did not knock, She strode in and shut the door behind them.

Karla opened her mouth to greet her, but Mrs. Soles raised a hand. Only, then, was Karla's fear confirmed: Mrs. Soles was not here on a friendly basis.

"I hear that you have seeing my son, Jake, outside office hours, are you two dating or something?" Mrs. Soles shouted at Karla in a fierce angry voice.

Karla just stood there looking stupefied at all this hostility from Jake's mother. She did not expect it. That does not mean that she could not imagine it.

"A woman of your---caliber does not deserve such a beautiful office. I will give you the credit though, you have maneuvered your way into one, anyway. I cannot even fault Jake." Mrs. Soles closed the distance between them in a threatening manner.

Karla was too shocked to feel anything other than the irritation and hate that highlighted every word out of Mrs. Soles' mouth. The way she said the words hurt Karla more than anything.

"If you really want your job, stay away from my son, Miss Bronson." Jane shouted.

"Stay away from Jake Soles. I will only warn you once." This time, she screamed.

Karla could only stare as Mrs. Soles turned around and walked away. Mrs. Soles did not waste words, but her words reverberated all over, leaving the room deafeningly quiet on her exit. It was not just her words, but also, the hostility in her attitude.

"Do not get close with the executives," George Bronson, her father, always said.

Karla had thrown this fatherly advice out the window.

8

MISUNDERSTANDING

Jake Soles swiveled his chair for the fourth time now. He was bound to get too dizzy soon. But he had already felt dizzy all day, just with thought. This may be too out of character for him. As the CEO, he has a stressful job, but swiveling in his chair may be too derivative, even when he is stressed. Sometimes to relieve stress, he would pour himself a drink in his office at midday or palm an autographed ball. It just means that he is worried about something. This fits into what we have learnt about him so far.

Just when all the pieces were falling into place, he remembered why he did not want anything to do with love, when he met Karla. He remembered Helen, the woman he had loved when he was in college. Helen was his first love. They had dated since their first year in college. She was beautiful and smart. They both wanted to be lawyers. She came from an equally wealthy background. It seemed like a match made in heaven. The only problem was that Jake woke up one morning and learnt that she had left him for another man. Helen stood him up on a dinner date. She just stopped answering his calls. She stopped texting him and refused to see him when he called on her. Nothing could have prepared him for the shock. Not that knowing the reason for such betrayal would have eased his pain, he wanted to know nevertheless, but it never came. It was like she disappeared into thin air. He lost his faith in women and has not had any sincere or lasting relationship since then.

Now, Karla was pulling away from him. That is the part that got to him, that it could be over soon after it really began. It was not long ago that they confessed their love for each other.

Or he was just overthinking it.

First, she texted to cancel a dinner date.

After that, Jake had invited Karla for lunch with him for three days, straight. Nothing seemed amiss when she had first said she was going to skip lunch for work and had not budged no matter how hard he had nudged.

The second time he had sent for her, she was not even in her office. After the third time, he began to worry that she was ill.

Jake Soles was not one to overthink. He prided himself on the fact that his thought process never exceeded logic or necessary questions.

Was there something she did not want him to know? He did not believe that that he had missed something. But then, what were the chances of that happening when he listened and watched her so keenly.

A knock on the door temporarily jolted him out of his thought.

"Come in, Karla," he replied.

His heart dropped as she stepped into the room, her stride causing her heels punctuate every step and every move. He could not help but notice that her hair had escaped her braid. He wished he could tuck it behind her ear himself. Her black dress hugged her shapely figure.

Her eyes glued to the file like they were the most important thing in the room. She was not chatty either, which was becoming the new normal. He opened his mouth to speak, still trying to figure out what to say but she broke the silence.

"This is the record for the Markoff case from last week. It requires your signature right there and we can mail it at once."

"Thank goodness," Jake replied. The case had been her constant excuse as to why she did not have time for lunch. Now they could lunch at least. He smiled up at her now. "You have spent so much time on that case. How about dinner together this evening, to celebrate?"

"Celebrate?" a smile teased the corner of her lips. "If I celebrated for every task I completed, that would be extremely expensive."

Jake kept hope alive.

"You know what I mean, Karla. So, as soon as we get off work? Dolores?"

"I am sorry. I will not be able to make it today either. I have work I am lagging on, and it will be due soon."

"My work? I do not think there is anything due that soon, Karla," Jake said. There was worry in his voice.

"I am your Paralegal/Secretary, Mr. Soles."

Jake shut his eyes, exasperation setting in. She reverted to formality. He had told her to call him 'Jake.' She had been calling him 'Jake' and suddenly it was back to 'Mr. Soles'? When he opened his eyes, he did not mask the emotion he was feeling.

"You do not need to remind me of that, Karla. I know you do work for the junior associates when there is time.

Did you take something else on?" This may fit the line of questioning when he asked if it was work for him that she must do.

"I am not. Being your Paralegal/Secretary is my priority. If more assignments come up outside this, I am sure I would love to do my best on them too, sir. But there is a ranking for now."

Jake stared at her, speechless. Where was all of what she was saying coming from? It was unwarranted. For goodness' sake, they had put aside the formalities when they were alone, at least. They had even confided in each other about personal things. They have even confessed their love for each other. Now one morning, she had arrived at work determined to put it all behind her.

Was she blind to the fact that he needed her? That he missed her company. Surely, it was not that.

He swallowed up the next words he had planned to say and only replied, "Okay, Karla. If you have a moment to spare any of these days, please ring a friend. You have my home line. I will be happy to spend time with you," Jake said.

Karla gave a small polite smile, a nod and then she was gone, moving as fast as she could until she was behind her own door. Only then did she allow herself to lean on it and heaved a sigh of relief. Jake still had no idea what had happened. The innocence in his eyes every time they met, and the hope that this time she would agree to go out with him, was killing her. Karla wanted to. She wanted to spend time with him so badly. Considering his mother's hostility towards her, Karla was ashamed of how much she missed his company. Each time, a little piece of her seemed to leave too with his dashed hope.

But she was not a match for Mrs. Soles. Often, after the

day Mrs. Soles had spoken to her, Karla wondered what she had been thinking, getting so close to Mr. Soles the way she had.

Had her parents not warned her to stay away from people like him? Why had she not listened?

A call interrupted her reverie. It was her brother, Zach.

"Karla, do you have time to talk? It is urgent," Zach said.

"Alright, Zach. I am busy with work right now, but you can come to meet me after work. I should be closing soon and then we can talk," Karla said.

"Then, I will be on my way. Let us grab a bite to eat, too," Zach said.

After the line went dead and a little more sighing, Karla dragged herself over to her seat to begin to get ready for work's end.

Jake Soles did not see a need to stay longer after he finished work. Usually, he was the last to leave as he always had so much work during the day: appointments, discussions with staff and other lawyers, conference meetings, and reading and signing documents. Since Karla worked overtime too, they had grown accustomed to meeting at the close of their day and spending the time together.

As soon as he finished and had pushed thoughts of self-pity away from his mind. He walked out of the office and into his car.

He turned up the car's music and sang along, trying to clear his mind. It was going fine when his eyes casually brushed over Dolores and stopped at the people behind the first window.

He saw a man in deep conversation with Karla and laughing with her.

Karla seemed happy.

Jake let a sigh escape him.

He could not get a full view of the man from where he was, but he saw him reach out and tuck Karla's hair behind her ear. He watched Karla lean into his touch and suddenly, all the pieces began to come together.

The man was obviously special to Karla.

Did she not say that she was busy?

But who is he? Karla never mentioned him, Jake wondered.

Now he could not help wondering if she had only responded to him because he was her boss and not because she was genuinely developing feelings for him.

It took him all he could to tear his eyes away and drive home. The last image of her talking and laughing with another man, after being so non-communicative with him for a while now, doggedly stayed in his mind.

9

THE TRUTH

Mr. Soles learnt that his son, Jake, worked from home for two consecutive days. Absenting himself from the office was not at all like Jake. Jake was very resolute. He stayed in the office and made sure things were running smoothly.

So, when Jake had called in sick the first day, Rodney Soles had wondered if his son was okay.

He was in his study the day Jake had pulled in from work before his unexplained hiatus. The study gave him an unobstructed view of his house, from the entrance gate to the main residential building.

He had been reviewing documents all day and looked up only because he had heard the car. He watched Jake slam his car door hard. Jake visits his parents regularly in the Santa Monica Mountains, a beautiful mansion where he lived since childhood. After he became the CEO, he bought a beautiful house by the waterfront, in Santa Monica, about fifteen minutes from his parent's mansion.

On this day, Jake just collected documents and left, as he was not in the mood to speak to anybody.

His father, the Chairperson, Mr. Rodney Soles, understood from the company secretary that Jake had not been to work for two days in a row.

Rodney Soles let himself settle for the suspicion he had that Jake had just found out what his mother had done.

Rodney had told his wife that it was a bad idea to go to Jake's girlfriend to tell her off for hanging around Jake. He had tried to tell his wife that there was a possibility that the girl and Jake were in love and her action would only hurt Jake's feelings.

She had gone ahead anyway. Now the consequences were beginning to show up. Rodney had thought that Jake was doing fine and had almost believed that his wife had done the right thing. But hearing of Jake's absence from work for no obvious reason for the past few days showed him that either Jake just found out or something else had shaken him.

Rodney did not have a troubled relationship with his son, but their relationship could be better. He regrets not spending enough time with Jake when he was young. At that time, he was the CEO, and he was busy. Rodney had tried to fill Jake's memories as much as he could when he was growing up, but there was only so much he could do. He missed not being able to attend his basketball and golf games and go fishing with him. That, however, did not disturb the relationship they had, and it was good enough, though they could be closer.

Rodney decided that if Jake did not show up at work the next day, he would have a talk with his son about things.

Jake Soles was not having a difficult day, he was having too many horrible days. It seemed stupid that he would avoid work because Karla Bronson was there, but he found himself doing it for the second day in a row. He could not even remember the flimsy excuse he left for his father as to why he was in a hurry and could not wait for a chat.

The only reason he had gotten out of bed even was because his stomach had been threatening to wring him to death if he did not eat anything. So, pancakes it was, because Karla Bronson had been serving them at breakfast and Jake has gotten to like them.

The thought of that, of Karla, made him lose his appetite after three bites. Ignoring his grumbling stomach, he pushed his plate away lightly and went to tuck himself under the sheets. He had had a tough time sleeping after the evening he had seen Karla at Dolores with another man.

All that evening, he had mentally turned the image of them over and over till it was beginning to mentally torment him. He let his mind picture them through the glass, the genuine smile on her face, the wrinkle in the corner of her eyes and the way her laughter must have rung out sweetly. He lived for her laughter and that beautiful, inviting smile that makes her face shine, which makes her so cute and desirable.

Imagine what had happened to his heart when he had seen her laugh that way with another man. He had threatened not to live again.

Jake sighed.

He was being too dramatic, in his own opinion, and for the first time in his life it seemed okay.

Rodney Soles called his son in the afternoon of the second day. He found it hard to wait till the next day. It was worrisome seeing his son whom he knew to be one to hold his head straight up in all situations, struggling hard not to lose his mind.

He had heard from the house housekeeper in his house that the boss had barely had anything to eat at all. He returned the food untouched. If he did touch it, it was not more than a bite or two. He was just living on coffee.

It took a while before Rodney intervened.

Rodney asked his driver to drive over to Jake's house.

"Let us take a walk," Rodney said.

Jake might have objected if his father had not already started walking.

"CBBR looks good in your hands."

Jake nodded. His father did not expect Jake to respond to his compliments with a "Thank you" because they were simply facts. It was helpful now considering that he was in no mood to hold a conversation. It had taken more than willpower for him to get up and walk out to meet with his father.

They walked for moments, not saying anything. Walking around the beach front was very soothing. It was heart-warming, watching children running around, people swimming and others playing in kayaks, while others were just sitting round with family and friends just enjoying the sea breeze and looking at the beautiful blue ocean. Jake wished he could be one of those carefree kids.

It was Rodney Soles again who spoke. "How is it going with CBBR? You know that occasionally I read what the books and the press say. I want to hear from you about CBBR. What is new?"

"Not much has changed except for new employees. The structures and strategies you put in place have barely changed. I am still watching the results of the changes you put in place. CBBR is standing strong now and it looks like it will be for a long time if nothing goes out of place," Jake said.

"Then why have you been avoiding it?" Rodney said

bluntly. He was a smart man but with his son, he was treading as carefully as he could.

Jake gave him a look and a raised eyebrow.

"I am sorry?"

"You heard me, Jake. You think I am blind?"

"I am taking a break from work. I deserve one. I have not taken a break in like forever," Jake said.

"Tell that to someone who does not know you," Rodney said.

"It is what it is, dad," says Jake.

"It is about that girl, right? Your secretary? Kim? Karma?" Rodney said.

"Ka—" Jake stopped, catching himself. He would not have fallen for that if he were thinking straight.

"Yes, that one. I know. We know about her," Rodney replied.

"There is nothing to worry about, dad," Jake said and wished hard he were lying.

"You are the CEO of CBBR, Jake Soles. The press has their nose in your personal business all the time. They have picked up stories of your office romance—." Rodney said.

"There is no office romance, dad. Karla is my Paralegal/Secretary," Jake said.

"I am not judging you, Jake. I am only surprised you are not mad at your mother. You have found a way to deal with your hurt well," Rodney said.

"Why should I be mad at mom?" Jake asked.

Rodney Soles frowned, now confused.

"It makes sense that you would. I told her not to go through with it. I was against it. She did not tell you about it so that makes it disrespectful. If what she did is okay with you then so be it. I am just saying you should not let it get in the way of your work," Rodney said.

But Jake Soles had stopped moving seconds ago. When Rodney looked, his expression was grave.

“What did mom do?" Jake asked.

Then it made sense to Rodney Soles that Jake did not know anything about it yet. It made sense that the girl did not mention any of what happened to him. Instead, she just withdrew.

He nearly slapped his head in realization. But Jake was impatient. He made him narrate the story in detail, mentioning how after his mother read the stories about his office romance in the papers, she had approached him, fuming, and threatened to go and tell her off. He watched his son's face harden with rage. He had not told him everything when Jake suddenly took off, running toward his house. He drove his car straight to their house and went straight to see his mother.

Rodney Soles could have sworn he saw tears in his son's fuming red eyes.

10

JAKE'S REACTION

Luckily, his mother was not in the house. Her absence averted a huge tantrum that evening. So, Jake left, frustrated and angry.

Jake was so downcast by the news of what his mother did that he locked himself up in his room the whole night. Everybody knew that Jake was stoic. Even his parents found it hard to read how he felt, but this time it was different. His father could visibly see the anger he felt. He now wished he had not told him anything.

"Jane, you always know how to push buttons." He muttered under his breath.

Heavy sighs kept coming one after another from Rodney, as his driver drove him back to their mansion.

Jake, on the other hand, could not have any of it. His mother surprised him with the extent she had gone to do such a thing. At the very least, she could have just inquired about the nature of their relationship before doing something that drastic. Not that he would accept her action even if she had inquired. He pondered about the humiliation Karla must have felt and how she would see him now.

Mommy's boy or did she now believe that I too saw her as a gold-digger? He had tried his utmost best to show her that he was not a bad person. Look what mom has done.

"What do I do now?" He asked the lifeless structures in his room.

His thoughts running from pillar to post, his mind still enkindled in anger. The harder he thought, the more the memory of her beautiful smile in that restaurant kept reoccurring in his mind. If only he saw the face of that other guy, he would know if he was worth it. Then he changed his mind. No matter how he looked, he would not accept it.

He was sure Karla loved him first or loved him more. He wondered what he was thinking. He wants to be the only man in Karla's heart, full stop!

He marveled as to how she was able to maintain her demeanor at the office as normal as possible, not as normal as it was before the incident. She became too professional after the incident. He blamed himself for not being sensitive enough to have noticed that something strange was going on. He did not know what to think anymore, whether it was because of his mom's tantrum or because of that *'other guy.'* He thought he had gotten close enough to her. Now she saw the way his mother must have painted him, 'out of her reach.' That single act has messed everything up for him. To think that she now thinks he sees her as a gold-digger and a fraud. Who knows what kind of words mom used on her.

He decided to dust himself up and get back on his feet. He vowed that no matter what it will cost him, he must make things right.

It was Monday morning and the week kicked off with work as usual, but his reason for heading to the office that day was different. His eyes burned with a different kind of fire, the one of determination.

That morning, Mr. Rodney Soles called Jake to check up on him.

"Decided to go to work today?" he asked, a new magazine in his grasp. He was sitting in the parlor, with his legs crossed and a cup of coffee comfortably sitting on his side table.

"Yes, Dad."

"Stop by for breakfast," his father said.

By the time Jake arrived, Mr. Rodney Soles' chef had already served a specially carved breakfast: caviar, lobster, omelet, cream, chives, creamed spinach, and lobster sauce. There were pancakes, Yukon gold potatoes and all sorts of fruit juices.

"Well, you are in a rush, sit down and have breakfast. I asked the chef to make a good breakfast because your housekeeper has informed me that you have not been eating," Mr. Rodney Soles said to Jake.

"I do not know, I have a tight schedule today," Jake said.

"You are the boss of the enterprise. You can be late. You are not indebted to anyone," he elaborated.

He saw that his father was not going to give him the smooth sailing he had envisioned, so he decided to sit and have breakfast. Jake decided to eat a little. It is breakfast, he thought.

Rodney did not want to aggravate things any further, but it was something he must do. He took deep sighs as he watched his son have breakfast.

"So, what did you and your mom discuss?" he asked.

As he mentioned it, Jake at once halted the course of the pancake into his mouth. His expression became bleak and grim. He was strangely quiet and still.

"Jake?"

He pushed the food on the table aside and got up from

the seat. He pushed the chair backwards and walked to the exit of the house.

"Jake! You cannot keep doing this to yourself!" Rodney shouted before he slammed the door behind him.

The workday went as every other workday went in recent days. She was professional as she normally was and avoided even making small talk with him or even eye contact. Every time he tried telling her everything, it was as if something pricked his chest. The memory of her at Dolores was the height of it for him.

He got off work as usual and tried checking up on her to know if she was still at work. Unfortunately, she left the office earlier that day. He was heartbroken. He has been brokenhearted before, but this felt different. He could not decipher why he was feeling so down.

He decided to branch at Dolores before he drove back home. He unconsciously scanned the whole restaurant for a glimpse of her hair. He sat on the sit he and she normally sat at the place. He placed their regular order and kept gazing outside. That did not help. So, he decided to go to the park.

Jake understood that the ladies that claimed to love him were only after his money. But this time, the girl is different. He knew she was true at heart, and now, out of pain and humiliation she must have decided to date another guy instead of him. Something in his heart told him that Karla would not do that without even speaking with him.

His phone rang.

"Hello."

"Hey! Jake, honey, how have you been?" a female voice echoed from the phone.

"I am sorry, who is this?"

"Oh Jake, baby. It is me, Helen."

"Helen? Wha-what ar- why did you call? I thought you told your friends that you would never call me again," Jake said.

"I am sorry Jake. I was naive and immature then," Helen aid.

"Really?" Jake mockingly asked.

Jake was sitting on the bench at the center of the park. He was thinking about why Helen called him. They were once a thing. He saw people walking their dogs in the park.

A cab stopped in front of the entrance, the door opened and the leg that stepped out of the vehicle had a black heel on. It was Helen. She was wearing a baby blue blouse on a black skintight jean. She cat-walked towards him with a wide grin on her face.

"Jake."

"Helen."

They watched themselves in silence for minutes. Jake wondered how he knew where he was. He was not happy to see her. Their tale was one of pain and betrayal. Helen was Jake's girlfriend and soon to be fiancé. For no reason, she ended things with him. He was devastated and disoriented, and it was one of the few times that Jake had expressed his emotions. He loved her with all his essence, to the level that he was ready to do anything for her. He could not figure out why she ended things with him. In as much as he knew Karla was not in for his wealth, at that time he also thought that Helen loved him for who he was. But Helen turned out to be the boss gold-digger!

"I am sorry Jake. I was naive then."

"Naive? You did not seem naive."

"Look, you might not believe me, but I have seen that one does not value what he or she has until it is gone. I have lost mine, but I know I can get it back."

"I do not know what you are thinking Helen, but that ship has sailed a long time ago."

"Jake"

"I was ready to do anything for you. I-I, I was ready to make you mine forever Helen." Jake said.

She felt a cringe in her stomach. The idea of being a wife Is not important to her. All she wanted was money, *who cared about matrimony?*

11

UNEXPECTED VISITORS

Jake went home with things in his thoughts. His phone would not stop ringing. There were calls from different people. The most notable being that of his mother. He was disappointed by the fact that she was the cause of the current misunderstanding between him and Karla.

"What is Helen thinking? That I would take her back?" he muttered under his breath as his reflection glared back at him from the mirror. The vapor from the hot shower covered the mirror. He thought about all that had happened earlier that day. She dressed to catch his fancy, but he knew better than to fall for that.

His phone beeped and the interface displayed Karla. He had added a cure emoji and a red heart close to her name. He never believed he would do such a thing, but there he was, doing it. He rushed to answer the phone and picked up the call.

"He-hello Ka-" he tried completing his statement before his phone tried to slip off his grip. His reflexes were fast enough to dodge that problem. With little difficulty he was able to catch the falling phone midair.

“Karla?”

“Mr. Soles are you busy?” her cold tone sounded from the speaker.

“Sort of.” he said throwing looks around his bathroom. “What's up?”

“Well, it is the Eastern shore case. The client decided to drop out of the deal.”

“What! Why?”

“That reason is best known to him, but it is great relief for the company.”

“Well, no matter who it is, it is our motto to see every case to the end, an. indisputable fact,” Jake said.

The call went silent, and for a moment, Jake hesitated before breaking the silence with a hint of humor in his voice.

"Are you...," he paused, searching for the right words.

"If I am free tomorrow?" Karla playfully finished his sentence, her tone laced with amusement.

"You know me too well," Jake replied, his face lighting up with a wide grin.

She laughed, teasingly apologizing, "I am so sorry, sir. I have work to do."

"On a weekend?" Jake's smile instantly transformed into a sad expression. He was genuinely disappointed.

"There is just so much work to do, and you would not want me slacking, would you?" Karla playfully retorted, relishing the playful banter.

"Oh, come on, Karla," Jake's frustration became more evident in his voice, his playful tone giving way to genuine disappointment.

"I am so sorry, sir," she said, trying to be apologetic, her voice filled with amusement, and with that, the line disconnected.

Jake let out an exasperated sigh, realizing she had outwitted him once again. "She always knows how to keep me on my toes," he muttered to himself, a mix of frustration and admiration in his voice.

This time it felt like the entire world was crashing down on him. He at once concluded that it must have been that guy, he saw her with at the restaurant that was her "work."

He almost opted to skip having his bath. He had never felt this low, except since 'Helen." And thinking about Helen, her last statement resounded in his mind.

What did she mean? he asked himself as he took his bath.

It was like every other day of the week. The morning breeze was so cold it felt like razor slashes once it touched on the skin. Karla was still upset, and it was far more complicated because he had not figured out a way to explain matters to her. It seems like they are not even able to communicate any more, not even as friends. It did not exceed the morning greetings and frequent draft submissions.

There is a big strain on their relationship.

After the day's work was over, Karla had gone earlier than usual. Jake always assumed that she was with that guy again. This time he had vowed to make sure he saw them both to get a clearer look at the guy she had left him for.

He got off work and drove to their regular restaurant, Dolores, and watched outside from his car. His current positioning would give him a clearer view of the man if they showed up.

Jake wondered what he was doing. Was he stalking Karla?

"God, I must be crazy," he said to himself.

Two hours passed and there was no sign of either the guy or Karla. He just realized that he had become obsessed with her. His heart was longing for her but could not find her. That made it even worse. With a downcast demeanor, he returned to his residence.

On arrival, he could spot his mother's jeep and another unidentifiable vehicle parked beside it. Who could that be? Why is mom here? Has she come to apologize or make things worse than they already are? Different thoughts raced to and from his head. He parked his car and carefully walked to the entrance of his house. There was no one in the house but the housekeeper. He had not employed enough staff to take charge of the house so there was no one he could ask what was happening. The house housekeeper rushed to help him with his keys and work briefcase. She prepared his mind for what was waiting for him inside the building.

As he entered the house, the smell of coffee and pudding reached his nose and triggered his mouth to start salivating.

"Jake!"

His eyes were bloodshot at the mention of his name. His belly felt like it would twist in knots at that spot. He was about to turn to the source of the voice before the sound of his mother calling him halted him in his position.

"Jake Soles." This time he was clearly aware of who had arrived at his place.

He wished he could have just disappeared into thin air and avoided this.

"Mom. Helen?" he shouted.

"How was work?" Helen asked.

"It went as I had planned. And what brings you two here?" he asked, a couple of steps away from them.

"Come have a sit." Jane voiced, tapping the space on the couch on which she was sitting.

He sighed heavily, obliged, and sat down. She had a cup of coffee in her hand, and she crossed her legs. He did not want to obey but he did anyway. Afterall, she is his mother.

"Jake, you know I am your mother?"

"Yes." he replied coldly.

"And you know that I only have the best of intentions for you?"

"Really?"

"Yes, dear. I cannot stand by and watch you make the wrong choices." Jane said.

He was already fuming inside, but he controlled himself well enough to respond to his mother.

"So, I am not allowed to make my own choices, is that it?" Jake asked.

"I did not say that son. I am just watching over you sweetheart," Jane said.

"Mom! Mom! Please. That is enough. So why are you here? Cut to the chase," Jake said impatiently.

"You know Helen," Jane said as she stretched her arm towards her.

"Yes Mom, why would I not know her?" Jake retorted.

"Beautiful. You need to get married and settle down. Jake, as your mother, Helen is the perfect choice for you."

"What? You cannot be serious!" Jake shouted.

"Yes, I am honey, and she loves you. Not for your wealth, but for who you are," Jane said.

His eyes rolled and his stomach churned. He was fully aware that Helen was up to something. He just could not place his finger on it. He knew that Helen wanted something, but he never suspected it was his wealth.

Why would she have the audacity to go after his wealth

now? Did he seem vulnerable to her? What is she trying to exploit? She must have perceived a weakness in him. Jake's thoughts wandered all over the place.

"Mom. Helen and I broke up a long time ago. She broke up with me herself. So, I do not know what is going on," Jake said.

"She told me. But she was naive then. She was young. What did you expect from her then? She is now aware of her mistake and is ready to make up for it. Do you know what? I will let you both be. Talk things out. I will be in the kitchen." Jane explained and left the room for the kitchen. The sound of her heels receded, and the clock's ticking sound was oscillating.

Helen decided to break the silence.

"Look Jake. I am sorry. I am so sorry." Helen voiced and tried to kneel before him.

"Sorry? Helen, what did I do wrong?" Jake asked.

"Nothing, nothing. I was just a fool. I did not value what we had then, but it has dawned on me that you were the only one that gave meaning to my life."

Jake was amazed at her explanation. Goosebumps had already taken his skin in waves, but he was still as calm in expression as still water.

"I want to believe you Helen . I really want to, but you have done the deed." he said with his eyes closed.

"Jake, I-I need your help," Helen pleaded.

"My help?" Jake asked.

"Yes," Helen started shedding tears.

"Woah. Helen," Jake stood up and walked to her couch to sit beside her.

Jake is a tough one emotionally, but that did not mean he is stiff at heart.

"Jake." she said and held his hand. "Jake, I do not have

time anymore. If I do not receive medical help, then it is the end for me. You know how things have been with my family financially. Even if you are not willing to help me, I will be glad if you will only let me spend my last moments with you," Helen said.

"What are you talking about? What do you mean by 'you do not have time'? What did you do?" Jake asked.

"Promise me that you would be there holding my hand," Helen asked.

12

THE PROMISE

"Holding your hand? What did you do Helen?" Jake asked.

"Just promise me Jake." her eyes leaking fluids like a perforated leather bag.

"I cannot promise what I do not know about. You will have to tell me what is going on first before I can consider making a promise." he elaborated.

"You must promise me first, Jake. Please," Helen pleaded.

"God. Okay, okay. I promise," remembering how close they used to be, he promised in frustration. "What is the problem?" Jake asked.

"Jake."

"Mmmhmmm. The doctors have diagnosed me with cancer. An-," Helen said.

"What?!" He stood in shock. "Cancer?" Jake exclaimed in astonishment.

"Yeah," Helen answered.

"Since when? And for how long?" Jake asked.

"Well, the doctor said it is stage two breast cancer. He

said that if I do not receive medical treatment, I will not live long," Helen explained.

"Oh my God. Helen, I am so sorry to hear this," Jake exclaimed.

"No Jake. I am sorry," Helen said.

Jane walked into the room, tired of the boring wait in the kitchen, she came to quicken their discussion up a bit.

"So, Jake. What will you do?" Jane asked.

"What will I do? What do you mean mom? Am I a doctor?" he asked, astonished.

It was strange seeing his mother act all nice and caring towards a lady that wanted to get affiliated with him. Naturally, she would have scolded Helen and accused her of trying to siphon down his wealth. It then dawned on him that if his mother never did such to her, then she must be in support of Helen.

"What can I do to help a second stage cancer patient?" Jake asked.

Even though his relationship with Helen is over, he is not a cold-hearted person. He would help, out of kindness.

"Well, we can start with Helen moving in to stay with you, an-" Jane started to explain but Jake cut her off.

"Hell no! Move in with me? You must be absolutely joking." he said emphatically.

Helen started crying aloud, grabbing the attention of mother and son.

"Shh dear, take it easy." Jane pleaded.

"Oh my God." Jake bellowed with his palm on his face.

"She will move in with you and then, get the necessary treatments for her condition," Jane said as she seemed hopeful that she will succeed in her mission, after seeing how moved Jake was.

The room went silent for a while; the fake sobs of Helen was the only thing they could all hear.

"Mom, can I speak to you?" Jake asked.

"Yes dear, I am all ears," Jane replied.

"No, in private?" Jake said, his right brow raised.

"Okay." she turned to Helen, who was at that point trying so hard to be in character. "We will be right back dear."

They left the room and walked outside into the ornament garden. Expectedly, Jake was extremely annoyed. First, that his mother had ruined his chances with Karla, and second, because she had brought back a pain he wanted to forget.

"Why?" Jake asked.

"Why what?" Jane replied.

"Why did you say those things to Karla? Jake asked.

"Karla? Who is Karla?" Jane replied, feigning ignorance.

"Mom, stop acting dumb. Why?" Jake pressed for answers.

"Why should I not have said all I said? She was going after your wealth. I decided to let her know that I know since you could not see through her," Jane replied.

"And you could see through her?" Jake asked, bewildered.

"Clearly. She is a gold-digger and that is final," Jake's mother replied.

"Mom, you do not even know her," Jake said, his fingers pinching his nose bridge.

"Karmen, Karol or Karen whatever her name is, cannot be the cause of your demise," Jane replied, deliberately fumbling over Karla's name.

"Mom, listen carefully. I love you but I will not let you be the reason I am miserable. I do not love Helen. I used to love

Helen, but it is over. It was over a long time ago. She left me for another man. How could you, my mother, not understand how I felt and how I still feel?" Jake said.

"You do not know what is good for you, son," Jane said.

"There you go again! Stop treating me like a baby. I am a grown man for Pete's sake! I can make my own choices!"

"And I am your mother! That is what I do! It is final," Jane said.

Mothers can be powerful and can certainly influence their children. Jane's power is, however, more than that. She owns the majority of the family's share at CBBR. Jane's grandparents came from a wealthy family in Austria but fled the country to the U.S. during the cold war. They invested their money in Los Angeles real estate and stock market. Jane brought her inheritance to her marriage and to CBBR. This means that Jake cannot afford to be too nonchalant about his mother's opinion about who he marries, though she has not threatened him with withholding the expected inheritance, she is very influential among the CBBR Board members.

"You cannot be serious mom. Helen cannot stay here, never," Jake objected.

"Well, I have decided. You had better understand me. Plus, she is extremely ill, so she needs to receive medical treatment as soon as possible," she said.

"Then, why can't you and dad take care of her yourselves? It is not like she would disagree," Jake said.

"Well, we are not the ones that are going to be her partner." she replied and walked back into the house.

Blood vessels had already started appearing all around his face and neck. His hands rolled into fists and his face was red with anger. He clenched his jaw tightly, gritting his teeth in rage. He took deep breaths to calm his nerves. It seemed as if that technique would not calm him. He at once thought of Karla and his rage sizzled into a smile. He could feel his stomach flutter, as if butterflies were roaming free inside. The thought of her smile made goosebumps run over his arms and back. I really like Karla, he thought. Just that thought of Karla stabilized his emotions.

Finally calm, he walked back into the house. "If you are going to live here, you will obey the house rules." Not like there were any, but since she had connived to move in with him, he had to set up boundaries before things got out of hand.

"Su-sure." she answered as she sniffled.

Jane Soles only scoffed at her son and left her son and Helen in the house.

Since Helen had claimed she had cancer, she had to make sure her plans fall into place. She had employed people to ensure that everything seemed real in her attempt to get as much of Jake's wealth as possible.

Jake had insisted on taking her to the hospital to begin treatment for her ailment. In the guise that she already had her own specialist, she convinced him to join her to go to her specialist's hospital for her treatment. Jake was not convinced by her insistence to go to her own specialist. He suspected that something was off, but he decided on focusing on getting her treatment.

All he was concerned about was CBBR and Karla's thoughts towards him. They had arrived at the hospital and were in the waiting room with Helen at his side. If one could see her, one would believe Helen's act without a single doubt. She pretended to be terribly ill that even Jake did not notice.

His attention was on his phone. He was reading the earlier conversations he and Karla had before the tantrum his mother threw. He was even unintentionally smiling as they discussed. He never in his life believed he would be doing this, but here he is reminiscing over their conversions.

Helen figured she was wasting her time when she peeped into his device and saw him scrolling through pictures in his gallery. They were the pictures of him and Karla. They looked happy, genuinely happy. One would not deny that they both did look good together.

"The doctor may see you now." the gentle voice of the tall nurse called them back to reality.

Helen had swiftly looked away from his phone before he could notice the nurse.

"Oh. Thank you." Jake replied.

"This way please." the nurse directed.

Jake almost forgot that Helen had said she had cancer, and after walking a little ahead of her, rushed back, and helped her up.

Even though Helen's plan was to siphon Jake's wealth, she also wanted to enjoy herself. So, she enjoyed the care he gave her in their period together. They walked into the doctor's office. The label boldly plastered on the blue door was Dr. Eric Brown. After three knocks on the door, they heard a droning voice behind the door.

"Come on in."

They both entered, Jake, the gentleman allowed Helen to walk in first before he followed.

"Please have a seat." the man wearing glasses said, his right hand extended from across the table.

As Jake sat down, his eyes captured the fancy clock behind the doctor. It was exactly 1:46 pm.

"Good afternoon doctor," Jake greeted.

"Good afternoon, Dr. Brown," Helen greeted.

"Good afternoon Mr. and Mrs. Soles," Dr. Brown replied.

Jake coughed a bit when he heard what the doctor had said. Helen on the other hand smiled a bit.

"Helen. You are now ready for your treatment?" Dr. Brown asked.

"Yes sir. Thanks to Jake here," she said as she grabbed his arm.

"Ah, Mr. Soles. Thank you so much." Dr. Brown said as he stretched his hands towards him.

"No, no, it is okay. I am just being of help." Jake explained, trying to wriggle out of Helen's hold.

"Alright, shall we begin?" Dr. Brown.

13

MEDICAL EXPENSES

After the meeting with the doctor, they decided that she would begin medications as soon as possible, while they researched more for the need for surgery. For now, treatment would cost around $5,000 per month, rounding up to an estimated $60,000 in a year, and with the added expenses, everything totaled up to $100,000 per year. It was not a substantial amount of money for Jake, so he was willing to take care of the expenses. But in Helen's mind, a hundred thousand dollars per year was not up to the amount of money she targeted to steal from him. She had other better plans.

One would wonder why Helen who comes from a high-class family would be desperate for money from another man. Her family used to be noble and wealthy, but her family's company went burst about ten years ago and they have been trying to build back the company. That involved borrowing a substantial amount of money. The family name, however, is still respectable.

It was another day at work at CBBR and the atmosphere

in the office was so thick one could cut through it with a knife. William on his part was busy with office work, clients were just storming in and out of the building. Karla on her part had more grit than they would have thought. They had just finished meeting two difficult clients in a row, but her attitude toward them was what one would call true professionalism. Her perseverance and passion are every boss's dream.

"Ma'am please calm down; we will get your case sorted out." Karla's dulcet voice tried calming the raging woman.

"How can I calm down if you do not understand me?" the woman complained.

"But I do understand Ma'am. Okay, let us go over it one more time."

As Karla tried to explain matters to the pent-up lady, she heard a knock on the door.

"Come in!" She spoke.

William walked in. His tie loosened down to his third button. His hair was disorderly from the constant ruffling from stress.

"The boss is looking for you." he said to Karla and turned for the door.

She turned to the woman who was still red hot from anger because Karla had interrupted her session.

"I am so sorry Ma'am. I will not be long." she pleaded with the lady and headed for the door.

She closed the door behind her and took deep breaths. She was about to meet him again, so she had to be as calm and emotionless as possible. She headed for his door and knocked twice.

"Yeah, come in," Jake said.

She turned the knob to see her boss fully engulfed in

work. He looked even more handsome when he focused on work. He hung his coat behind his seat and beads of sweat were sliding from his forehead. The air conditioner was slightly malfunctioning. The service Department was already working on it. He looked sexy, even working in this stressful condition. His gaze was sternly at the computer monitor before him, and his eyes were making rapid movements on the screen.

"You called for me sir." Karla spoke, trying to remind him of her presence.

He was still grossly involved in the monitor before him. She did not complain. She used the time to fix her gaze on his great looks wondering how a man fully engrossed in work can be still look so handsome and charming.

He finally transferred his gaze off the system onto her beautiful figure. On landing on her figure, it stuck there, not wanting to leave nor blink. A slight smile crept up on the side of his mouth.

"Sir?" Karla called.

"Ah, I am sorry Karla. How far have you gone with the Gibson's case? He has been emailing nonstop," Jake asked.

"I finished that three days ago. I had drafted it for you this morning and left it on your table together with the other documents." she explained.

"Really? I did not see any Gibson's file on the desk this morning." he said and turned back towards the system.

"Sir? But" she paused and tried recalling if she really did place that document on his table.

Jake had paused already and looked at her from over the screen.

"I will go search for it now sir." she voiced and bolted out of the office.

"Take your time." Jake voiced.

With a soft smile on her face, Karla walked out the door. It then dawned on her that she had an unhappy client waiting for her in her office.

Could today get any more strenuous?

She rushed into the office and headed for the drawers of files lined up in the room. The client could not help but watch in surprise as to how Karla was sweeping through files at Godspeed.

"What about --?" The client was about to complete her statement before Karla raised her hand halting her instead.

She understood Karla's sign and decided to shut her mouth. Karla gave her a soft smile of appreciation and left with a file in a green folder. She left her office with the surprised lady inside and headed for Jake's office.

"The door is open." Jake replied to the three impatient knocks Karla gave.

She pushed the door and rushed into the room, placed the file on his table.

"I am so sorry for the inconvenience sir. I promise it will not happen again."

"Karla, it is okay. Calm down." he said with a smile.

"Thank you, Sir." she replied sternly.

He wanted to tell her to drop the formalities for the nth time, but he already predicted her reply and decided to just let it be.

"Is the recording from the last meeting with Gibson in the file?" he tried starting a conversation with her.

"Yes sir. I took the most vital information and left out the inconsistent ones like you asked."

"Alright. That is okay. Thank you," he replied and faced his system.

She was surprised he decided not to extend the conversation any further and got back to work. Being adept in the knowledge of behavior and expressions, she found it hard this time to read what was going through his mind. Her mind fluttered in thought before he raised his gaze above the system to see her figure before him.

"Any problems?" he asked.

"Oh, no sir. No. I will be taking my leave now." Karla replied.

He nodded and turned to the file, picked it up and faced his system. She left the room in confusion. What is with him today? Is he ill?

The day was already stuffy enough but Helen, who was oblivious of the fact that everyone was having a difficult day decided to take it to the next level. She arrived at the CBBR building and walked up to the receptionist's desk.

"Good afternoon miss. How may I help you?" the blonde-haired beauty asked from behind the counter.

"I am here on behalf of Mrs. Soles. Yes, you can help me. Where is the office of Mr. Jake Soles, the Chairman's son?" Helen asked.

The receptionist did not have a good feeling about letting her through, but the mention of "Mrs. Soles" gave her no choice.

"Oh, all right Ma'am. Let me call his office."

William was totally surprised that Helen was coming to see Jake. He knew that it was none of his business to get involved in Jake's personal life matters, but he needed to verify this.

As he was Jake's personal assistant, the call went to his office first. It is his duty to organize the bookings and meetings for Jake. He told the receptionist to stall Helen for a bit while he conferred with Jake.

"Today is one heck of a day." he muttered under his

breath as he placed the telephone back on the hook. He branched to Karla's office, whose hands were on her head trying to listen to the frustrated woman complain.

"Karla." William voiced.

"Yes sir?" the effects of strain in her voice.

"Please clear all schedules for the next two hours. It is one heck of a day." he said and turned for Jake's office.

Jake was already feeling the heat of the day when he heard a knock on the door for the nth time that day.

"The door is open." he voiced. He had removed his tie and unbuttoned his upper three buttons.

William pushed the door and stormed into the office.

"This Gibson's case is like a labyrinth. I can-" Jake was saying before William interjected.

"We have a problem," William said.

"Problem?" Jake asked, discerning William's frightened look.

"It is Helen." William uttered.

"Helen? What happened? Is she okay?" Jake voiced in shock.

William was surprised with the sudden statements of concern Jake said. "No, she is in the building, at the receptionist's desk," William said.

"What! Why? What does she want?" Jake exclaimed in surprise.

That is what I was expecting. I thought they were a thing, again. William thought.

"Well, that beats me. She insists on seeing you, and..." William paused.

"And what?" Jake asked, his brows deeply furrowed and his fingers pinching his nose bridge. One could tell he is annoyed and would get angrier if he went on.

"Sir," William said.

"William. And what?" Jake coldly asked.

Jake flustered William as he rarely called him by his name, and if he did so, it was not going to turn out well.

14

UNWANTED VISIT

"What the! Wah-wah," Jake yelled in anger and confusion.

That confirmed to William that they were not back together again. It was just Helen being unreasonable.

She really had to get it in her thick skull that Jake will not let her back in, ever. William knew about how Helen betrayed him and left him for another man.

"So, what should we do now sir?" he asked.

Jake heard three knocks on his door.

"Yes, come in," Jake said.

Karla walked in hurriedly. "It is the Gibsons on the phone. It is urgent," she said.

"Can they not have some patience." William voiced frustration.

"Let the call through. William, tell them to send her up."

"Yes sir," they both said in unison.

Jake slipped out a pen and paper and waited for his telephone to ring. He felt his eyes constricting and thought he needed coffee. He beeped for a cup of strong coffee and answered the phone.

Five minutes later, his door creaked open. Helen had packed her black hair into a ponytail and was wearing a black T-shirt over skin-tight blue jeans. She always has a thing for *@skintight wear.*

Jake was too engulfed with work to notice she had entered the office. He was working his keyboard and his other hand was holding the phone to his ear.

"What was all the wai-" she tried complaining before Jake raised his hand and signaled her to keep quiet.

"Yes Mr. Gibson. We will need more information on that sir... Yes sir... If we go for this case without concrete evidence, we will surely lose the case, and we both do not want that... Yes sir... We will need more time. Yes, you can speak with my assistant. All right sir."

His tired eyes gazed at Helen, who was sheepishly smiling at him.

"What do you want? Are you not meant to be taking your medications?" he said with a tired voice.

"Oh that? I am doing okay with that. So, why did I have to wait such a long time at the reception?" Helen asked.

Jake groaned in frustration, his eyes rested on the clock which read 1:22 pm. "Helen, I do not have time for this. Since you have taken all your medications for today, why do you not go home instead and rest."

"Well, I do not want to, I want to be with you here Jake."

"Helen, it is past my lunch break already, and I am having one heck of a day. So please if you do not mind, could you please go home?" Jake pleaded.

"What do you mean by that? So, I cannot have lunch with you?" Helen argued.

The mention of her having lunch with him made him think about the various lunch breaks he and Karla used to have. He then decided that he must have lunch with Karla, no matter the cost.

"Are you seriously telling me to leave your office?" Helen asked.

"No Helen, I am asking you to." Jake corrected.

"Is that so? Because of that girl who works for you?" Helen asked.

"Helen!" Jake screamed. "Watch what you say about her, or else. Now get out," he almost screamed.

Helen was so embarrassed and in shock that she unconsciously backed out of the room and found herself in front of his door. She turned in anger and her eyes landed on the door with Karla's name on it. She decided to go and infuriate Karla but was disappointed because Karla's office was not open.

"Has she left already? She is so lucky," Helen muttered to herself.

She vowed to return and finish things up with Jake and Karla later.

It was already 1:45 pm and Jake had just finished all he needed to do in the meantime. He tried to see if he could take Karla to join him for lunch, but she had gone before he could reach her. He was not ready to give up and instead decided to go to their favorite restaurant for lunch. He hoped to find her there.

It was a short drive to Dolores. All Jake had wanted was to see Karla and talk things out. He entered the building, and he scanned through the restaurant, searching for Karla, but she was not there. He was now down casted. He considered giving up, but he decided to go and sit at their regular spot and reminisce.

Karla left the office earlier to meet up with a friend of hers, Ingrid. She has been friends with her since childhood. They grew up in the neighborhoods of South LA together. Luckily for Ingrid, she had left the neighborhood after receiving a scholarship to study abroad in England. She had graduated with honors and got employed in the city of New York. She came to address a business forum in LA and decided to catch up with her old friend, Karla.

"So, you mean to tell me that Jake's Mom said all that?" Ingrid asked.

"I was as surprised as you are, and she was not joking when she said that stuff. I just do not want issues."

"So, you are avoiding him. How is that going?"

"Very badly. We meet each other every day during the week at work, so it is inevitable," Karla said.

"So, what do you do then?" Ingrid asked.

"I just keep everything between us at the professional level. I do not even stay around for short conversations. I do not even allow eye contact," Karla said.

"Really? Does he know?" Ingrid asked.

"Know what? What his mom did or that I am not talking with him anymore?" Karla asked.

"Well, both." Ingrid said, using her hand to move the strand of hair on her face.

"Well, I do not know if he is aware of his mother's actions. But by now, he must have noticed my sudden change of attitude towards him," Karla said.

"Well, I pity him though, poor thing," Ingrid said.

"I should be the poor thing," Karla retorted.

They both laughed. They had a cup of coffee each at the coffee bar. Ingrid had to catch up with her conference for the evening and bid Karla goodbye. She was going to stay in the city for a while since the conference would last a week.

They bid farewell and were about to go their separate ways before Ingrid offered to give Karla a drive to the restaurant Dolores first.

Jake was already playing with his salad with his spoon. He was hungry but he seemed to have lost his appetite. He was facing the window, so he could see the vehicles that had come into the park and those that had left. He was staring into the window, his eyes keenly searching for Karla, hoping she will show up.

Could the other guy have picked her up or is she at another place?

The sight of a lady whose hair was like Karla's almost made him spring up from his chair. He looked carefully at the face and figured it was not Karla, but one random person.

A Toyota Prius drove into the lane and stopped. He squinted his eyes to see clearly. There were two women behind the dashboard, and one of them was Karla. His heartbeat started racing and he could feel his mood brightening. He unconsciously stood up, his gaze on the lady who was leaving the car.

He could not wait anymore and decided to walk out of the restaurant to receive her himself. She had packed her hair into a bun, but her hair was still sticking out.

"Hey," shouted Jake, just as Ingrid drove off.

Karla shuddered out of shock. She turned to see who it was, and her eyes widened in surprise and fear. "Mr. Soles!" she voiced.

Karla could sense something was off. She was not staring at him in just mere shock. He could see she was afraid. Is she now afraid of me? Mom, see what you have done.

He then decided to make her feel at ease. "Karla, are you okay?" Jake asked.

"Sir? N-n yes sir. I am okay." she stuttered.

"Karla, please we are no longer at the office. You could drop the formalities now," Jake said.

"Well, it is just lunch break, we would soon be back at the office," Karla replied.

"Alright, all right, you win. May we go in?" Jake directed.

Has he been waiting for me? Karla wondered.

"Yeah, we may," Karla replied.

Guess it is a date. Jake thought.

They both walked to the table they used to sit at every time.

"So, what would you want to eat?" Jake inquired.

"Sir? I will have anything available," she replied.

Jake knew she was lying. She was normally the one suggesting their meal every single time they went out for lunch.

As soon as the waiter left with their orders, Jake took a deep breath and leaned towards her.

"Karla," Jake said.

"Yes sir," Karla replied.

"What did I do? Did I hurt you in any way? I feel like I did something wrong, but you do not want to tell me." Jake said, in a bid to make her speak up.

Karla hesitated and then replied. "No sir. You did not do anything wrong to me."

"So, tell me, why has your attitude towards me changed these past few weeks? I thought that we were heading somewhere. We even confessed our love for each other. What happened?" Jake asked.

His phone began to buzz on the table, he looked to see

who was calling, it was Helen. What is her issue now he wondered?

He then declined the call and put his phone on airplane mode. He then looked back at her and smiled, “Talk to me.” he said.

15

THE CONVERSATION

"There is nothing I can tell you Jake. I just do not want your Mom to end my career," Karla said.

"I knew it! It was my Mom," he voiced.

She was surprised with the ferocity of his response. All she had was her job and her family. The idea of Mrs. Jane Soles ending it all sent shivers down her spine. She could gladly say that she tried avoiding her son. She also did not reveal anything about what she said to him. She knew he meant her no harm whatsoever and that he would never think of doing her any harm. All she was afraid of was just Mrs. Sole's threat and if ending her beautiful relationship with Jake Soles was going to let her keep her and family safe, then that is what she must do.

"Look, Jake. I do not want any problems. Your Mom had sternly warned me to stop being around you," Karla said.

"But I like being around you Karla and I like you by my side," Jake said.

"But everyone else thinks otherwise," Karla said.

"Everyone else is not us, Karla. Are we going to listen to

them and let their views direct the course of our relationship?" Jake asked.

"But..." Karla was starting to say.

"But what Karla? What?" Jake replied.

"They all think I am pursuing you because of your wealth. Jake, your mother called me a gold-digger. Everyone else thinks the same. I do not want to drag my family to the mud. We do not need to go any further down," Karla said.

"Let them think what they may. What matters is that we know that we love each other and why. It is out of the pureness of our hearts and mutual admiration for each other," Jake said.

"Jake, look at me. I am not in your class, neither am I worth all the attention. I really appreciate that a man like you can love me. For me, it is a dream come true. However, I do not want to hurt anyone nor let people have a bad impression of me because of how I feel about you," Karla said.

"Karla, look, I have had friends and acquaintances in this life of mine. You are the only person I have been this free and comfortable with. I value our friendship and our love. I know what I love about you. I do not care what other people think or say, be it my Mom or the public, I do not care. If class were my priority, we would not have even been here together. So please, do not let me go," he said and grabbed her hand.

He was completely honest with her. He had never been this close with anybody as he has been with her. There was just something different about her that he loved. Whenever he was with her, he always felt the presence of a certain sincerity, purity, and peace. He always felt at ease with her. Jake believes that Karla is the one. His instincts told him never to let her go, no matter what.

"But your mom," Karla asked.

"I cannot even imagine the hurtful things my mom must have said to you for you to ignore me the way did. I am sorry. I apologize on her behalf. From now on, leave my mom to me, let me deal with her. Let us just get back to how it used to be between us," he pleaded, grabbing her hands in a plea, while gazing into her eyes.

Members of the paparazzi had already recognized Jake and had taken pictures of him holding Karla's hands. The two of them were only aware of themselves, the surroundings to them were like blurred sights and sounds. The only thing that mattered to them both was just them both.

"Please Karla, stop calling me Mr. Soles, it makes me feel like my father. Do you not think we have past that stage? Let us just stick with our names, Jake, and Karla, at least outside the office," Jake said.

She laughed hard, something he had not heard in a long while. The sound of her laughter was like a melody. He wished she would feel like that every time. He had achieved his aim by making her comfortable around him again. So, Jake leaned towards her. He used his left hand to fix a loose strand of hair on her face. He held her hands in his and looked straight into her eyes and said, "Do not run away from me. I have already fallen in love with you." She nodded.

Their meals came. They enjoyed the food, chatting with each other the way they used to.

Jake was extremely proud of himself for making such progress with her. He seized the opportunity to tell Karla of his Mom's and Helen's plans. He assured Karla that he would take care of both.

His thought was to find a way to settle Helen, because she, more than his mother, was the big threat to his relationship with Karla.

The next day, Jake's mother stormed into his house in anger. She was furious with the news flying around the net. The photo of him holding Karla's hands, both looking into each other's eyes and the punch line that he was dating her, infuriated his mom. Jane considered all the methods she would use to frustrate Karla. Not going for Karla first, she opted to confront her son to demand answers. She must clarify her plans for him.

Her entitlement as his mother drove her to plan her son's life the way she felt was perfect for him. In her plan, Karla was not the suitable one to be at Jake's side, so she was ready to fight tooth and nail to end whatever they had together. Jane arrived at her son's manor like a tsunami. The workers in the house, some of whom came from the Soles' mansion, dreaded her. She was not a bad person. It was just that she was the type who stood strong in her thoughts and has a way of making people around her feel uncomfortable.

Rodney, her husband, had warned her not to go ahead with her rampage, but she just knew how to ignore advice. She met her son. They had a nuclear argument. She tried making Jake understand that Helen was the right person to be his wife and not Karla.

In arguing for Helen, Jane considered her family background, both families were top Los Angeles socialites and that her Mom was her good friend. She wondered how she would interact with Karla's parents. They have nothing in common, in terms of wealth, education, or social class.

"But Mom I do not love Helen, I do not even like her. I am interested in Karla. I love her!" he tried explaining.

"Interested? What do you mean by 'interested'? And get that idea out of your gear. Helen is the one for you. Love? It is Helen who loves you, so do not mess this up," Jane said.

"Mom, I would rather die than have anything to do with Helen. I am paying her cancer bills from the goodness of my heart, nothing more."

"Karla is the problem, right?" Jane asked.

"Mom! Do not dare lay a finger on Karla. She has nothing to do with my decision. I pursued her. I was the first to love her. I was the one who made friends with her. I was the one who took her on dates, I was the one who took her to the beach. She does not deserve any of this from you. Please let her be. The threats you unleashed on her were enough to almost end our budding relationship, but no more Mom. I have had enough of your *desire for perfection* in everything," Jake said.

Jane was so shocked that she left Jake's house with mouth agape. Her son's level of independence dawned on her. She was far from giving up but was impressed that her son had enough grit to talk back at her in the manner he had done.

Helen 's demand for the payment of her medical bills was getting suspicious. Jake had used the communication that opened between him and Karla after their last meeting and explained the Helen situation to Karla. He asked for advice on how to manage the situation. She advised him to hire a private detective to figure out what Helen was up to.

The private investigator that Jake hired to spy on Helen brought back crucial information about Helen. To Jake's amazement Helen proved to be a fraud. Even Jane Soles and Rodney Soles admitted that Helen was not who they thought she was. She was never sick nor ill. She was just in the search for a means to drain money off Jake. Jane found it hard to believe that Helen could do this to her and her family after what she did for her.

She thought it was one of Karla's strategies to paint

Helen black, but Jake explained that it was not so. The private investigator expounded the information he got from spying on Helen Frazier. He disclosed how Helen had employed various persons to make her scheme of having cancer seem real. How all the money Jake paid to the hospital for her treatment was transferred to an offshore account she had created. The private investigator also disclosed Helen's detailed plan to extort Jake by siphoning more money from him.

Out of anger, Jane tried calling the police on Helen, but Jake prevented her from doing that. Everybody now knows her plans so she had everything to lose. They called her to the main house and showed her all the information they had gathered about her and asked why she did all she did. All she could do was ask for forgiveness and pardon. She insisted on returning all the money she had stolen from them, but Jake asked her to keep all the money she had fraudulently taken from him and never return to his life again. This decision was based on Karla's advice.

Jane in as much as she never liked Karla, had to admit she was smart. Jake had grown up in opulence and wealth. Since childhood, his parents taught him that even though he was born into riches he had to work for everything he earned and wanted. His parents had raised him with upright morals and even though his family was not religious, they always distinguished between right and wrong. Rodney was the most open-minded one in the family. His open-mindedness was what made him the successful man he is today. CBBR was like their second family. Rodney and Jane worked there till their retirement. Their son who had graduated with honors took over the management of the family business and brought it to the great heights it has reached.

One time in middle school, Jake had taken his classmate's property without his permission. He was young then and he liked the toy. He had been asking his parents for one of those, but they had said that if he got good grades in his tests, he would get it. When they found out about that. They waited until he got those grades, got him a similar toy, and told him to give the new toy to the kid he had taken the toy from.

It was one of the few ways they taught him how not to transgress. Thanks to their method of discipline, he had set his mind for perfection in everything that he did. Helen's behavior was so disgusting to the Soles that they expected her to pay for her wrongdoings.

One thing the Soles were guilty of was that they never forgot a wrong, and that totally rubbed off on Jake. As an intellectual, he analyzed everything, and most times he always tried going through events in his head. Rest assured, his former life with Helen and how she dumped him for no reason always came back to haunt him. He had not forgotten nor forgiven, but Jake was a good man at heart.

If there was a thing Jake Soles was afraid of, it was his heart and the emotions he felt. Most times he did not know how he would control them or how to expel them, but his great intellect allowed him to mask them. Karla was adept in knowledge of how to read his emotion from his eyes. All the ladies he had dated never saw through this. They were too blind by their won selfishness to notice it.

His love life with Helen was a mess. An absolute hell! She used emotional threats to manipulate him. He had never felt so stupid and used in his life. He just could not understand how his mother thought she was the right choice for him. She was clearly a liar and a fraud. What made her dump him then was what he never knew.

Thankfully, that is in the past now.

16

RIDDANCE

Jake and Karla finally rid their lives of Helen, and by doing so, they eliminated the major hindrance to their love. But they still had to pacify Jane Soles, who for no reason would not accept Karla as a good person. She was going to be the major setback to their future union.

Jake had thought about his life with Karla and had seen that she was the only suitable person he could share his life with. He had grown to love her for who she is, and for all she is. Her morals excelled and he loved her wit. He was ready to advance their relationship to another level by proposing to her. He knew that his mother would be against it, so, instead he approached his father for advice.

Rodney was not a man who looked at people's class or background. He was the most open-minded in the family and would readily give his son the advice he needed when he needed it. So, he drove over to their family mansion.

“Dad,” Jake called after he sat down.

“Yes son.” Rodney answered, wrapping the newspaper he was reading.

"Could I speak to you about something important?" Jake asked.

"Well of course, you have all my attention," Rodney answered, giving him all his attention.

"Dad, I came to you because you are the only voice of reason here. Mom is too blinded by social class to give me any reliable advice," Jake said.

Rodney laughed a bit and took a sip of his whiskey. "Want some?" he asked Jake as he stretched the glass towards him.

"Yes dad, thank you." Jake replied, taking the glass of liquor, and taking a sip.

"I understand that your mom is not right in the actions she has taken," Rodney said.

"I know. Thanks dad," Jake said.

"So, what is it that you wanted to talk about that you cannot discuss with your mother?" Rodney asked.

"Well, uhm, da," Jake mumbled.

"I know where this is going. Is this about Katarina?" Rodney asked.

"Dad, her name is Karla, and yes," Jake said.

Rodney smiled and took another sip of his drink. "Do you love this lady?" Rodney asked.

Beating him to the chase, Jake was surprised with the forthrightness of his father. "Well, I have thought about it, and y-yes, I think I do," Jake said.

"You think. You do. They are two different things you know" Rodney asked.

"Well, dad. I love her. I believe that she feels the same way about me," Jake said.

"Look son, if you could have the series of arguments you have had with your mom for her, then you really do love her. That is clear even to an old man like me," Rodney said.

"But what about mom?" Jake started.

"Jane is my wife. You do not need to worry about her. I will take care of her. You do what you must do," Rodney said.

"Thank you, dad," Jake said.

That afternoon, Jake took a friend of his, Stan, to one of the most opulent jewelry shops in the city. He wanted the engagement ring to be perfect. He wanted to make it all memorable for her. He wanted to get her the perfect ring that would make her face glow in surprise on seeing it.

Stan was a man of class and opulence. He had exquisite tastes in ornaments, precious stones, and metals. Jake needed his ability for the perfect engagement ring for his bride to be. He had tried to sound her to predict the exact type of ring she would love. All he worried about was what her reaction to his proposal would be. He had heard her countless times say that she was not of his class and just somebody from a poor home. From his knowledge, she was the one supporting the family financially in a major way. He knew she had a sense of responsibility, which might be the reason she would be hesitant to accept his proposal. He did not want to rush things, so he asked her out first.

"I would like to go out with you, Jake. I am just afraid of what your family might say," was her reply to Jake asking her out.

But the thought of that guy he saw with in the restaurant after his mom's tantrum kept bothering him.

He took her to La Angelique Restaurant, one of the fanciest restaurants in Los Angeles. La Angelique Restaurant, is known for its warm atmosphere, cordial service, and nice food. Jake made the reservation a week in advance. As they entered the restaurant, a beautiful well-dressed service staff took care of their seating. Another staff took care of their drinks and menu orders. They were all cordial and polite. Karla enjoyed the cozy atmosphere.

"Karla, could I ask you something?" Jake asked her as they had their dinner in the fancy eatery.

"Yes of course." she said and took a spoon.

"On the day that I signed the Markoff case documents, and you gave me a lecture on your job as a Paralegal/Secretary," he was saying before Karla paused for a while, "you had gone to Dolores for dinner," Jake said.

"Oh yes, I did go there for dinner. Any issue?" Karka asked.

"I saw you there, with, with one other guy. And he was touching your hair," Jake said.

"Oh, you mean Zach?" Karla asked.

"Yeah, he is my brother. He had something important to discuss with me then. I even had to buy him food." she said and laughed a bit.

Jake also laughed, but not at what she said but at his stupidity. He wanted to knock his head with his fists. He calmed himself knowing and just admitted he had made a mistake. He had wrongly suspected that Karla was seeing another man. He should have had more faith in her. He should have known that a woman with her sincerity would not immediately start seeing another man after their love confession for each other, irrespective of his mother's behavior.

It was a beautiful Sunday evening, and Jake had picked Karla up after church that day. She was wearing the red dress he recently bought for her. No one would deny that that dress suited her. Her black stiletto heels beautified her legs. She styled her hair beautifully that night. It was as if she took her time to do that. Bangles adorned her hands.

The night sky was mesmerizing, and the romantic lighting in the place accentuated her beauty.

"Karla," Jake said.

"Yes Jake."

Jake looked deeply into Karla's eyes. The weight of his emotions evident on his face. He took a deep breath and finally broke the silence.

"We started as boss and employee. Then we became friends. And a wonderful thing happened. We fell in love. Now we are dating," he began, his voice filled with sincerity. "I bless the day I met you and thank you for being with me and for accepting my love."

Karla's face lit up with a huge grin, her eyes sparkling with affection. She could not help but respond in a playful yet heartfelt manner.

" Jake, I love you, and I promise you that not even a herd of rampaging llamas or a sale at my favorite shoe store will take me away from you," she exclaimed, her voice brimming with humor.

Jake's expression turned from one of pure adoration to a mixture of surprise and amusement.

"Llamas and shoe stores, huh?" he chuckled, shaking his head in disbelief. "Well, that is good to know. I will make sure to keep an eye out for those sneaky llamas."

Karla giggled, wrapping her hands around his. "You never know when they might strike, Jake. We must be prepared!"

They both burst into laughter, reveling in their shared lightheartedness and the joy of being together.

Both Jake and Karla are happy that they have restored their relationship to what it used to be. The havoc Helen created is now behind them. They now trust each other.

Jake was aware that he must meet her family and introduce himself. After that, the task of getting his mom on board would be next.

He was not able to get the rest of his sentence out. He had been dating her, but he still got tongue tied when he saw her all dressed up. She drove him wild. Always have and always will. He wanted to hold her and tell her how beautiful she looked. He wanted her to know that she was the most beautiful person in the room. He pulled her close and whispered into her ear, "You are the most beautiful woman I have ever met. And the sexiest. You look so good in this dress, but I cannot wait till I get to take it off you." Karla giggled and wrapped her arms around his neck, "Hey! You are so naughty. But thank you baby, I love how hot you make me feel."

They talked about everything. Jake loved that he could share anything with Karla, and she understood. She always had the best advice, the best stories, and the best reactions. She was a perfect listener, and he was always happy when they were together. She was the perfect company, his perfect company. He wanted no one else but her. She was everything he ever wanted, and he wanted to spend his life with her.

Jake watched as Karla throw her head back in laughter as she talked about the show, she had been watching the previous night. He always listened to all she had to say because he wanted to know everything about her, all her favorite shows, all her favorite things. And that was because, she never hesitated to tell him about anything. She was an open book; one he was glad to read.

Karla noticed that Jake had just been staring at her for a while, "Baby, is something wrong? You have not said anything for a while now." Jake broke into a smile, "I was just admiring you. I love you and I would rather watch you talk about the silliest things than be anywhere else. There is nowhere else I would rather be than right in front of you, staring at you, lost in the magic that is you. I love that this is my life. I love that I have you and I never want to know what it feels like not being with you" Jake said and immediately got on one knee. Karla gasped and placed a palm over her mouth.

Jake continued, "Ever since the first time I woke up to you touching my chest, accidentally" they both laughed, "I have known that I only want to spend the rest of my life with you. You make me so happy, Karla. There is no one else I want to cook for, massage her feet, take out to the beach, but you. I want it all with you. Life will never make sense, if you are not right next to me, living it out with me," Karla had tears of joy streaming down her face. Jake brought out the box from his jacket pocket and asked, "Karla Bronson, would you be my wife?" She nodded her head enthusiastically. He happily slid the ring in her finger, and she jumped on him, planting kisses all over his face. He hugged her and held her, whispering sweet promises to her. Then he kissed her with such longing, showing her that he would always want her, every minute of every day.

"Wait, you never said 'yes'," Jake broke away from the kiss. Karla laughed and lightly hit his chest, "Of course, it is a **YES.**" I love you Jake and there is no one I would rather be with, I want to share my life with you, till death do us part." Jake gave her a long lingering kiss.

It was the best day in his life. He had engaged the love of his life.

Karla followed Jake home and he wasted no time in touching her. He kissed her while grabbing her waist. He walked her over to the couch and laid her there. He planted kisses all over her neck and went down to her cleavage, planting wet kisses there. He loved how she tasted. He pulled open her top, exposing her lace bra and he looked at her and kissed all of her. Karla began to moan. She needed him to taste her. She drove him wild, but he was about to drive her to the wildest point. He dipped his head down and tasted her. She moaned loudly till she reached the height of passion. He remembered his promises. So, they enveloped themselves in each other's arms. She had expressed her desire to go all the way with him only after they had married, and he respected that. So, they just stayed cuddled in each other's arms, enjoying their cozy love.

17

JAKE MEETS KARLA'S FAMILY

Jake wanted to meet Karla's family first. He wanted to become familiar with her family members, her friends, where she grew up. He hoped and prayed that her parents and her family would approve of him. Jake wanted to know everything about Karla.

He was driving down now to the place where Karla grew up with her family. It was where she still lived. It was quite a long drive from where he lived.

"I am beginning to wonder how you make it to work so early every day," Jake said as he turned a bend. Jake preferred to do the driving himself, especially when he was with Karla.

"It is a crazy run for the bus. Thankfully, there are people who prefer to sleep some more and would rather race for the second bus," Karla said.

"Do you want a driver or are you willing to do the driving yourself?" Jake asked.

"I do not know how to drive," Karla said.

" I will come pick you up then," Jake offered.

"Every morning?" Karla asked.

" You bet," Jake

Her eyes were full of gratitude and Jake hated that he could not sink into them for just a moment because he had to focus on the road. He reached over and squeezed her hands.

Karla frowned.

"Are you nervous?" She asked.

"A little. I have never met your parents and your siblings. I am known to have a bad first-time meeting with Bronson's," Jake said remembering the events of Karla's first day at work.

"Technically, I am the only Bronson you have met," Karla chuckled remembering the first day she met him.

Jake made a face. "Also, I have something big coming up and that is scaring the crap out of me."

"What is that about? I thought we sealed the deal with Roberto. That is the only important thing you mentioned so far."

"Things could be different. Thank you, Karla, for bringing that contract for my golf match. CBBR would have missed it," Jake said. It was the third time he had said it to her and knowing that Jake had not grown up that appreciative, made her swell with pride for him. They were both learning and relearning, not just about themselves but what life on the other side meant.

During the drive to Karla's place, they discussed the poverty in her neighborhood. She told him of increasing poverty rates on her own side of the world and of how some people made do with makeshift shelters on that side.

Jake had heard poverty stories as CBBR frequently donated to charities. However, this was the first time it was coming so close to home. He had found that there were places that charities did not get to. The claim was that the

NGOs did not distribute the donations in an equitable manner, and they favored certain areas. More people need help than charity foundations could aid. It was also difficult to register all the people who need financial support for such aid.

Karla's part of L.A. was that part of the town where they retired to struggle not to drown.

"Are you nervous?" Jake asked. "You are quiet."

"Even when I was a high school cheerleader and popular, you were not in my wildest dreams. This was not," she gestured at everything with a wide sweep of her hands, "You were not. I know I dreamt big but not as big as you. It is overwhelming now and sometimes I pause and pinch myself to make sure this is not a dream. It is crazy. You are crazy to love me. Now you are heading to my house planning to tell everyone that I am your fiancée. Such dreams were out of bounds to any girl with the life I come from."

Jake found a way to pull her into his arm, while keeping one hand on the wheel. He kissed the top of her forehead.

"I dreamt of what we are. I dreamt of finding a woman that would be in synch with me, that would be my heart's desire. But even my imagination did not paint it this beautifully. You brought life to my heart's desire, and I am thoroughly in love with that and in love with you. For me, it is a dream come true, " Jake said.

He planted another kiss on her forehead and focused on the road again.

They were there.

Karla's side of South L.A was not too far from the entrance and soon, they had come down to walk the remaining distance because the street was too packed for cars to cross.

Karla had always wondered what kind of man she would

bring to meet her parents where they lived. She wondered if she would be embarrassed and shy or feel vulnerable. But now, hand in hand with Jake, she felt comforted and felt trust tune the beat of her heart. Though he walked silently beside her, she understood what he communicated with his hands.

They squeezed hers when his heart went out to the people who were cowering away from him and those who were indifferent. Jake, she noticed, had tried to dress to blend in as much as he could. He knew they did not know who he was. It was obvious to everyone that he was not an ordinary man.

Jake squeezed her palm again when he saw how he fascinated the children. She comforted the tremor that reached his hands and recognized the stiffness to his body. He could not believe this was what it was, what it looked like. Not too far away, a dog barked wildly, chasing after a cackling chicken.

"This is home," Karla said, stopping in front of a small bungalow. A teenage girl sprinted out of the door and collided with Karla, nearly knocking her down.

It was Karla's little sister, Gwendolyn.

Jake began to meet the family. Jake met with George and Priscilla Bronson, Karla's parents, her sister, Gwendolyn and her brother, Zach. Naturally, they were so curious about him. Jake found George to be deeply knowledgeable and well spoken. That is not strange as most Reverends are. Karla's mother was on the quiet side. He thoroughly enjoyed their company and Karla's family loved him. They discussed about the poverty situation in South L.A. George explained that the neighborhood has known better days. Gradually, over the years, affluent people exited the neighborhood to places like Hollywood and its suburbs.

By the time it was evening, and Jake was leaving with Karla, five charity organization projects were already set up for South L.A.'s low-income neighborhood. Jake had donated to the community and had arranged for meals and shelter for multiple families.

George and Priscilla Bronson, alongside their remaining two children stood and watched them walk away, waving. Karla, of course, was going to be back later that evening, but for now, the beach was waiting for them.

As soon as they entered the car, Karla broke down with emotion. Jake held Karla while she wept, overwhelmed again by how far she had come. Jake had promised that CBBR would officially partner with different organizations to deliver the much-needed help in other communities in other places in LA South.

Karla soon recovered. At the beach they watched the sunset in companionable silence. Jake was jealous of the way Karla liked to take in the view. In another life she must have been a good painter. In this one, her cup drawing on the sand looked like a bird.

"You are my dream, Karla. Not for any reason other than the fact that I could not see myself wearing the shoes I do now. I did not know Jake Soles this way. Oh, I got around with different girls all right but not one of them made me want to keep her forever. Forgive my choice of words, Karla."

She did not need to, she understood him perfectly. When Jake was being raw with words or emotions, she saw the part of who he used to be, a remnant of his change. He was still in the process, and she found that beautiful to watch. How he now took extra care of his choice of words in order not to offend. It was not something he had cared to do when he first met her.

"With you, it is different. It is like you are a song I find relatable, and I want to play over and over and make my friends listen to it, yet I hallow it and my ears swear never to get accustomed to it. You make me want to talk with all the words in the world even when I need just a few words for you to understand."

"So, you want to play me. Hmm, should I be worried," she put her hand on her hip, and grinned at him.

He moved closer from where he had been standing, pulled her up and wrapped her in his arms. She felt the thud of his heart and wanted to sing to it and wanted to tap his chest lightly to the rhythm. He kissed her, and said, "I love you, Karla, with all that I am. It is hard to believe that you are not in my earliest memories because it is like you have been there all my life. I want you to be with me for that long anyway."

18

THE PLANNING

It was a wedding preparation that brought together the Brunsons and the Soles. Once the couple set the date to marry, everything began to happen all at once.

First the meeting of the two families over dinner at the Soles' place. The members of both families were nervous that day. They tried not to be. They had every reason to be. Karla wanted her parents to make a beautiful first impression. She remembered what it was like, her earliest memories with Jake. How she had to learn so many things that she did not know because of her background. She did not want her parents to look any less to the Soles, especially Mrs. Jane Soles. Jake had left the task of convincing his mom to accept Karla to his dad who had promised to do so.

Karla, though she had forgiven Mrs. Soles, could not help being wary of her. Mrs. Soles had standards she did not compromise for any reason. It was something to be wary of because they seemed to be everywhere, even down to family mealtime.

Jake had tried to run Karla through the ones he remembered growing up and Karla had added the information to the ones she had learned from her own experiences with Mrs. Soles, and she had told her parents of them.

Mr. Rodney Soles was less trouble to deal with. He was easygoing and open to diverse conversations and ideologies. He and Mr. George Bronson had easily struck a cordial note, engaging in conversation, discussing topic after topic, sharing laughter over drinks.

Jane Soles had been absent that day. She had excused herself with a prior scheduled meeting. Before she left after Karla arrived, all she did was give Karla basic instructions, "Keep your shoes right there," "I will prefer that you stayed away from that room", "The boys are looking for you."

Rodney Soles had apologized for his wife's absence and promised that she was going to be present on the day to pick out a wedding dress.

Karla wished she were not there. Jane Soles was particularly difficult.

"That gown is a petty thing to wear on your wedding," Jane said, "it looks like it was taken off a display mannequin."

Karla found the gown pretty enough. It accentuated her waist and was easy to move around in. Jane disapproved of every dress Karla tried. Yet, she was the one who chose the shop.

"I think the dress looks beautiful, Karla," Karla's mom, Priscilla Bronson said, a smile spreading across her face.

Jane snorted. "You need to see better. You cannot wear that to wed my son, the press would have a great weekend."

"I am willing to try any dress you pick, ma'am," Karla told Jane softly. She was being particularly calm for her own sake. She could see that all this was already frustrating her mother. It was the first time the two women met. Priscilla was getting irritated with Jane.

When Jane finally picked out a dress, Karla thought she would choke in it.

It was as though she had wanted Karla to look like what she had first called her. The dress was trampy, open in four places.

"I cannot wear this, ma'am. It is not a proper thing to wear to a church as a bride," Karla said.

"Why are you going to a church?" Jane asked.

Karla knew what was coming if she answered the question. She knew that Mrs. Soles did not approve of them being married in a church. To her, a wedding at their home or a destination wedding is much better. Church weddings were too concerned with being prim and proper to let the couple have any fun on their day.

"Can I have adjustments on this dress?" Karla asked the attendant. Hopefully, if she agreed with Mrs. Soles' choice of dress and added her touch, they would come to an agreement.

The attendant nodded. The arguments between Jane and her mom had also stressed her out.

"We will return then," Jane Soles said. Karla raised a brow. "It will not take long to get it done, ma'am," she said. The attendant nodded again.

"Yes, but it is time we get to the venue arrangements," Jane Soles said already halfway to the door.

"Mrs. Soles, would it not be better to get this over and done with?" Priscilla asked. Despite her mother's calm tone, Karla knew the strain she was under. If she ever came back here, it would not be with Jane Soles.

"My mom can be particularly difficult; we both know that. But it is your wedding, Karla, it is our wedding. We will not allow to make everything go her way. I trust you; I trust your judgement for our wedding. We can talk about anything, and our decision would stand. I know we are coming from two different sides of the world but that must not stop us, yes?" Jake had told her that the morning before they went shopping for dresses.

If choosing a wedding dress was tough, making plans for the wedding itself was much worse. So much effort went into making weddings happen beautifully, Karla was only just understanding and appreciating that.

The Bronsons wanted a church wedding and wanted to invite people from their church. Members of the church George Bronson had served at as a Pastor were eager to watch his daughter get married. It would be better not to slight them by not inviting them as they contributed to Karla's development. They taught her at Sunday school. She also taught younger children Sunday School. She had collaborated with them when they did church events such as bible studies, block events and fund-raising drives to mention but a few. She had learnt things from them.

The Soles did not see the need for a big wedding. They preferred a simple affair for the families and friends. They did not want too much attention from the press, knowing what that could turn into.

Once again, the difference in their backgrounds played the devil's role in their relationship. The CBBR executives were already too much of a crowd to invite, alongside both families, in Jake's opinion.

But the Bronsons knew the church was more than just people they met in a building. The church was an extended family to them. It was where Karla had grown up too, where she had learnt her values.

"A church wedding and a destination wedding is too much celebration and will be an unnecessary duplication," Jane Soles had remarked when Karla had raised the idea of having two weddings so that they could meet the needs of both families.

Though her method of expressing her opinion was never polite, Mrs. Soles was not wrong. It was hard enough to organize one wedding.

"Jake and I should talk about this and get back to all of you. I am sure it will be easier for us to get to a great solution that way than for all of us to decide on what we have divergent view on," Karla said.

In the end, Karla's suggestion calmed the tempers that were quickly rising. Jake stared proudly at his brave and smart fiancée.

"I am glad you are managing this so well. My mom can easily scare people away," Jake said.

"She is being protective, I understand her. Your mom will like us later. She just needs to be convinced that her son is in safe hands," Karla said.

Jake leaned over and kissed her lightly on the lip.

"I cannot wait to be married to you. I do not care who is there and who is not there. I do not care if we exchange vows in a church, in my family house, on a treetop, or on San Mateo-Hayward Bridge. You will be my wife and I can barely wait for that."

Karla laughed.

By the end of the day, they had not yet come to an agreement. But they were not in a hurry, the wedding was a couple of months away. They will figure things out.

Jake Soles was the man God had designed for her. He is her destiny. It had not looked like that at the beginning. Then he was just her smart, handsome, rich boss, but the end was coming together beautifully, and she could not wait.

19

THE WEDDING

It was a beautiful spring day, the sun was shining, and the birds were singing. The wedding day had finally arrived, and Jake and Karla were excited. They had been waiting for this day for months, and now it was finally here. Jake and Karla's love was as strong as ever. The Bronson's and the Sole's family came to an agreement to have a church wedding and not a destination wedding or the two. The reception will take place at a nearby reception center. "Karla and I have made our decisions and we think that this is the best way to accommodate people we invite and make things easier for us" Jake said to both families at the last dinner meeting they had two weeks before the wedding day. "What about the crowd and the press that will be involved," Mrs. soles asked with a frowning face. Jake knew that his mom was not happy with the decision to have a church wedding. "We can take care of that mom, it is not much of a big deal," said Jake.

Mr. Rodney Soles stood up and took Jane outside of the house to talk to her. "Jane, please let Jake do what he wants to do. This is to the benefit of both families. Karla and her family will become a part of us soon and we cannot start this new Union with fights and quarrels. Just let them do what they think is right, Karla deserves to be happy," Mr. Rodney said.

The whole plan was already set within two weeks. The plan was to have a proper wedding at the altar and a reception at a nearby venue not too far from the church. The attendant amended the wedding dress that Mrs. Soles picked for Karla. Karla put it on, and it was elegant.

Karla's church was always special to her. She had wanted to get married there ever since she was a little girl. On her wedding day, the church looked even more beautiful than she had ever imagined.

Karla was stunning in her wedding dress chosen by Jane for her. The shop attendant had adjusted it to fit her perfectly. Jake looked handsome in his black tuxedo. They had planned everything down to the smallest detail, and now what remained was for them to say their vows and become spouses at the altar.

The audience was large as the two families had invited their guests. Jake was not concerned about the crowd anymore because he wanted to please Karla and make her happy on their wedding day.

Finally, the moment arrived. Waiting at the altar was Jake, dashing as ever, in his elegant, black tuxedo. Karla was beautiful and radiant as ever. As soon as they started playing the wedding song, her father had walked her down the aisle to the altar, where Jake was already anxiously waiting for her. As soon as he saw her, his face beamed with joy.

As they stood at the altar, looking into each other's eyes, they knew that they were meant to be together. They had been through so much to get to this point, but they had never given up on each other.

The bride and groom exchanged their vows. It was full of beautiful moments, from the exchange of vows to the lighting of the unity candle. And as they exchanged rings, Jake and Karla looked into each other's eyes, promising to love and cherish each other for the rest of their lives through thick and thin, in sickness and in health.

The pastor pronounced them, husband, and wife.

Finally, they became spouses. They shared their first kiss as a married couple. All the guests stood up and gave them a resounding applause. Karla felt like she was on top of the world. It was joyous.

They had made it to this point, and now they were ready to start their new life together.

Karla's heart was beating fast, and she felt tears of joy prickling at the corners of her eyes. She was finally marrying the love of her life, and she could not believe how lucky she was. Her boss became her love, her destiny.

The celebration that followed was nothing short of incredible. Jake and Karla made their way out of the reception center, greeted by a flurry of applause and cheers. As they walked down the aisle, the couple looked at each other, smiling with sheer joy and happiness. Outside, a flurry of confetti rained down on them, and it was like a sea of smiling faces greeted them.

The reception hall was beautifully decorated. The organizer did an excellent job decorating the wedding reception center, with a combination of eclectic table décor, magical lighting of assorted colors, with flowers, confetti, and candles everywhere. The guests enjoyed a delicious feast of food and drink. Jake and Karla shared their first dance, swaying to the music with their arms wrapped around each other. Friends and family followed suit, taking to the dance floor, and enjoying the festivities. The guests danced and had a wonderful time.

Jake and Karla made their way to the reception hall after meeting outside the hall to greet the CBBR executives who came during the celebration at the reception center. They apologized for being late. They explained that a drunk driver hit their car on their way to the church. "Was anybody injured?" Jake asked with a worried expression on his face. "Not at all" they replied. Karla sympathized with the CBBR executives for the accident and the executives. Jake, and Karla, all went back to the reception hall where they ate, and they danced the night away. They laughed and they shared their love with everyone around them.

As the night went on, the couple found themselves alone, in a quiet corner of the reception hall, Mrs. Soles interrupted. "Congratulations my daughter-in-law" Jane said as she handed a glass of wine to Karla. "Thank you, ma," Karla replied with a smile on her face. Jane walked out and winked at Jake smiling at both. Jake and Karla looked into each other's eyes, and they knew that they had fulfilled their love in every conceivable way.

They embraced each other, their bodies wrapped in an intimate embrace. They shared a deep kiss. They knew that they were meant to be together, and they were determined to make every moment count.

As the night ended, the couple knew that they had started their new life together in the best conceivable way. They had fulfilled their love, and they knew that they would continue to do so for the rest of their lives.

The celebration was already ending, Karla and Jake had

one last dance together. They looked into each other's eyes with deep love and appreciation. The guests formed a circle around them, clapping and cheering as they shared this special moment. It was a day that Jake and Karla would celebrate forever, a celebration of love, family, and friendship that had touched everyone's heart.

It was the best day of their lives.

They arrived home as a married couple. He had fulfilled Karla wish not to sleep with her until after the wedding.

There is now nothing stopping them. Now he is Karla's and Karla is his. Jake wasted no time in pulling her towards him and carrying her in his arms into their bedroom. He gently caressed tiny strands of hair on her face and pushed them back while looking loving into her eyes with all the desire a man can have. He kissed her full on her lips, while grabbing her waist. He carried her over to their wedding bed, and gently laid her on it. There were beautiful petals red roses on the bed. Karla looked at him with such desire, longing and waiting for his touch. He planted kisses all over her neck and went down to her cleavage, planting wet kisses there. They had waited for so long for this day. He loved how she tasted. They could not wait any longer. They both tore each other's clothes apart. They simultaneously reach for each other's lips, teasing and then passionately kissing each other all over. Karla began to moan and said, "I love you, Jake." She needed him to taste her. She drove him wild, but he was about to drive her to the heaven of love. He dipped his head down and tasted all of her. She moaned loudly till she climaxed on his tongue. She reached her hands towards him and touched him till he shared the same fate. Since they had waited so long Karla had expressed her desire to only sleep with him after they had married and

Jake as a gentleman had respected that, their passion for each other on this wedding was beyond normal.

They continued to enjoy their love and passion until they were exhausted. They cuddled into each other's arms, united as they slept.

It was a beautiful wedding day!

20

THE FUTURE

After the wedding, Karla moved into Jake's house, a beautiful house by the waterfront, about fifteen minutes, in Santa Monica. It was also close to work. No more waking up at sunrise and racing to catch the early morning bus.

Karla loved the house, but she also felt a little intimidated by the opulence of it all. Its decor and the number of staff working in the house overwhelmed her. There was a chef, a housekeeper, and a gardener. She had grown up in a low-income home where her father's income as a gospel preacher was not even enough to feed the family of five and supply all their necessity. She had never experienced such luxury before. Her mother was a stay-at-home mom who did all the shopping, cooking, and cleaning. Karla realized that she may not need to lift a finger in her new home. It is a new lifestyle of managing the staff that she must get accustomed to.

Jake had grown up in a large house with servants, and he was accustomed to a certain level of luxury. The servants dealt with Jake's needs. He sometimes struggled to adjust to doing things for himself.

The first few weeks of their marriage were a blur of unpacking boxes, decorating their home, and settling down to their new life as a married couple. They both had busy days working together in CBBR and often came home exhausted, but they were always available for each other. During the week, Karla chose the dinner menu and left instructions about the dinner with the chef. During the weekends, Karla, and Jake cooked dinner together, watched movies, and cuddled on the couch. Sometimes they went to the beach or ate out at their favorite restaurants.

But as the weeks went by, Karla began to feel like an outsider in her own home. She felt like she did not belong in Jake's world of luxury and privilege. With time, challenges surfaced. They realized that they had different ideas about how to spend their free time. Jake liked to go out and socialize with his wealthy friends, while Karla preferred to stay at home and spend time with her family. The problem is that now she is married it will not be appropriate to continue spending time with her family.

They sometimes argued about how to spend their weekends, and it led to tension in their relationship. She felt like she was living in a bubble, disconnected from the real world. She missed her family and friends back home and felt guilty for wanting more.

One evening, she sat Jake down and poured her heart out to him. She told him how she was feeling and how she missed her old life. Jake listened patiently and held her hand, reassuring her that they were in this together. He told her that he loved her for who she was, not for where she came from or what she had. He promised to support her and help her adjust to their new life.

From that day on, things got better. Jake tried to introduce Karla to his friends, and to involve her in his activities like his golf and basketball. He took her to fancy restaurants and art galleries, and to local markets and street fairs. He wanted her to experience everything the city had to offer, but also to stay true to her roots. Karla immediately made a friend in Jake's circle. Her name was Jackie. She was the wife of one of Jake's friends, Jared Thomas. Jackie admired Karla's personality very much and took her under wing. Through her, Karla met other friends in Jake's circle. She joined them to organize things like barbecues and went shopping with them. Karla was reluctant to buy expensive beautiful things. They assured her that it was okay. They told her that now she is married to Jake, she must dress elegantly.

Jake and Karla also made a conscious effort to compromise and meet each other's needs. Jake tried to be more involved in the household, and Karla tried to go out more and socialize. They discovered that they could both learn from each other's backgrounds and experiences. They realized that they could build a life that incorporated the best of both worlds.

Karla embraced her new life with a newfound enthusiasm. She learned how to cook fancy meals, how to dress for formal occasions, and how to hold her own in social gatherings. She bought fashion and catering magazines and educated herself. She also taught Jake how to make her favorite dishes, and how to appreciate the simple things in life.

It was not easy, but they managed to cope and adjust to each other's differences. Their biggest challenge showed up as they got more accustomed to each other. Karla had always dreamed of having children, but after months of trying, she was still not pregnant due to a medical condition and Jake had never imagined that they would struggle to have children. Each negative pregnancy test result was a blow to their hopes and dreams. It was not easy on both as they passed through the challenge of childbearing. "What do we do, Jake" Karla asked with tears in her eyes as she leans on Jake's shoulder. It is already one year and three months of marriage without pregnancy. But even as they faced disappointment, they were committed to each other and determined to build a life together. Jake keeps consoling Karla assuring her that they will give birth to a child one day.

Jake and Karla consulted a fertility specialist. After tests, he informed them that they might not be able to have children naturally. This was devastating news for them, but they did not give up hope.

They decided to explore other options, talking to doctors, and considering fertility treatments. And through it all, they supported each other with unwavering love and compassion. They eventually decided to try In Vitro Fertilization (IVF). It was a long and complicated process, but they were determined to have a child together. Finally, after rounds of IVFs, Karla became pregnant. It was a joyful moment for them, and they looked forward to a happy future as a family. As Karla's pregnancy progressed, they faced new challenges. Karla was often tired and uncomfortable, and Jake did everything he could to support her. He rubbed her feet, cooked her meals when the chef was off, and made sure she had everything she needed.

And when their baby finally arrived, Jake and Karla could not be happier. It was a boy and they named him Alexander. He is fondly known as Alex. There was this feeling of overwhelming love and joy everywhere. They took turns holding their precious baby, marveling at the miracle of new life. As they navigated the challenges of parenthood together, they knew that they could face anything if they were together.

As they faced the challenges of parenting, Jake and Karla were always there for each other. They worked as a team to raise Alex and to build a happy and healthy home. They knew that they must have each other's back, no matter what life might throws at them.

As the months went by, their love for each other grew stronger. They faced challenges, but they always worked together to overcome them. They learned from each other, supported each other, and never gave up on each other.

Their love story was a beautiful example of how two people from diverse backgrounds could build a life together based on mutual respect, love, and determination. They were each other's rock, and they knew that no matter what life threw their way, they would always have each other.

As they looked ahead to their future, Jake and Karla were excited and hopeful. They knew that there would be more challenges to come. They also knew that they had the strength, the determination, and the love to face those challenges together. They were grateful for each other, and for the life they had built together. They were excited to see what the future held for their family.

They had so many dreams and plans for their life together, and they knew that anything was possible if they were together. And as they held hands and looked out at the city skyline from their balcony. They knew that they were exactly where they were meant to be.

Of course, Karla wants another baby, a girl. Jake wants to take the family to Paris on vacation. There are so many things they want. They are now confident that they can do them all.

Jake and Karla's story was a testament to the power of love and commitment. They had overcome obstacles, but they never gave up on each other or on their dreams. They had built a life together that was based on love, trust, and mutual respect. And as they looked to the future, they knew that they had everything they needed to face whatever challenges might come their way.

They marveled at their beautiful billionaire tantalizing workplace romance.

MY NEXT BOOK

Did you like this book? Then you will LOVE my next book, "**HATE YOU TO LOVE YOU.**"

Enemies to Lovers Romance.

My parents' failed romance still taunts me.

Now I see every woman as being interested in my bank account.

That is until I met her. They call her Adriana Anderson.

For the first time in more than ten years, a woman ignited my heart.

Her beauty is exquisite: dark, lush hair and a thin, beautiful mouth, cat-like eyes, arched brows, and milky skin.

Then I listened to her speak.

We could not be farther apart on issues about women.

My greatest desire turned into a nightmare.

Yet, I yearn for her.

Trevor

He is too handsome for real life! Too irresistible!

The moment I saw him, my feet got rooted to the ground, and my heart skipped a beat.

But handsome, arrogant, powerful, Hollywood star, Trevor Tudor, believes that all every woman wants is money.

I am a civil rights activist. I agitate for women's rights.

This heat surging between us is dead from the start.

We are already enemies.

Adriana

Start reading "HATE YOU TO LOVE YOU" NOW!